BIG GHOSTS DON'T CRY

A BEECHWOOD HARBOR GHOST MYSTERY

DANIELLE GARRETT

Copyright © 2019 by Danielle Garrett

Cover Design by Melody Simmons

Chapter Art by Fred Kroner Stardust Book Services

All rights reserved. No part of this publication may be reproduced, distributed or transmitted in any form or by any means, including photocopying, recording, or other electronic or mechanical methods, without the prior written permission of the publisher, except in the case of brief quotations embodied in critical reviews and certain other noncommercial uses permitted by copyright law.

Publisher's Note: This is a work of fiction. Names, characters, places, and incidents are a product of the author's imagination. Locales and public names are sometimes used for atmospheric purposes. Any resemblance to actual people, living or dead, or to businesses, companies, events, institutions, or locales is completely coincidental.

BOOKS BY DANIELLE GARRETT

BEECHWOOD HARBOR MAGIC MYSTERIES

Murder's a Witch

Twice the Witch

Witch Slapped

Witch Way Home

Along Came a Ghost

Lucky Witch

Betwixt: A Beechwood Harbor Collection

One Bad Witch

A Royal Witch

First Place Witch

Sassy Witch

The Witch Is Inn

Men Love Witches

Goodbye's a Witch

BEECHWOOR HARBOR GHOST MYSTERIES

The Ghost Hunter Next Door

Ghosts Gone Wild

When Good Ghosts Get the Blues

Big Ghosts Don't Cry

Diamonds are a Ghost's Best Friend

Ghosts Just Wanna Have Fun

Bad Ghosts Club

Mean Ghosts

SUGAR SHACK WITCH MYSTERIES

Sprinkles and Sea Serpents

Grimoires and Gingerbread

Mermaids and Meringue

Sugar Cookies and Sirens

Hexes and Honey Buns

Leprechauns and Lemon Bars

NINE LIVES MAGIC MYSTERIES

Witchy Whiskers

Hexed Hiss-tory

Cursed Claws

Purr-fect Potions

Furry Fortunes

Talisman Tails

Stray Spells

Mystic Meow

Catnip Charms

Yuletide Yowl

Paw-ful Premonition

Growling Grimoire

MAGIC INN MYSTERIES

Witches in the Kitchen

Fairies in the Foyer

Ghosts in the Garden

HAVEN PARANORMAL ROMANCES

Once Upon a Hallow's Eve

A TOUCH OF MAGIC MYSTERIES

Cupid in a Bottle

Newly Wed and Slightly Dead

Couture and Curses

Wedding Bells and Deadly Spells

CHAPTER 1

When you're a ghost whisperer, friends don't expect you to bring wine or a decorative candle to their housewarming party. Instead, they expect you to come prepared with a stockpile of sage, a five-pound bag of salt, and an iron poker. They will happily feed you appetizers in exchange for a thorough paranormal inspection and the subsequent exorcism of any wandering spirits.

Hey, it beats being asked to lug boxes around on moving day.

So, when my boyfriend, Lucas, invited me to come see his swanky new condo in downtown Seattle, I packed accordingly. He'd been moved in for a little over a week, but I hadn't yet been able to make a getaway to see it in person. Seattle was a three-hour drive from Beechwood Harbor and required a little bit of planning, considering I owned and operated a flower shop.

"I came bearing gifts!" I announced, handing him the bag of salt when he opened the front door.

Laughing, he took it from me. "I thought you were kidding about this."

"I like to come prepared," I teased. "Aren't you curious to see if you have any invisible roommates?"

He mulled it over as he opened the door and ushered me into the condo. The unit was in a swanky, high-end building with spectacular views of the city and waterfront. The corporate rental was only meant to be Lucas's temporary digs until he could find his own permanent residence in the city. In the meantime, it was good to enjoy the high life.

"This view is ridiculous!" I exclaimed, stopping in front of the wall of ceiling-to-floor windows. In keeping with the condo's minimalistic theme, there weren't any window treatments. Nothing but sparkling skyline, glittering under the hazy moon.

"I'm not missing the two-star motels the studio used to put me up in, that's for sure," Lucas replied, crossing the room to stand beside me. He smiled at me and then looked out the window. "I've been to Seattle several times, but it looks different somehow."

"Like home?" I ventured.

He looped an arm around my waist, drawing me closer. "It's starting to feel that way," he said, giving me a meaningful look.

"Oh! Speaking of, I come bearing gifts," I said, reaching into the canvas bag slung across my chest. I pulled a gallon-size glass jug out and presented it to Lucas. "A growler of that beer you like at McNally's."

With a wiggle of his brow, he took the large bottle. "Now it's a party."

"And my shoulder is celebrating," I teased. "Between the bag of salt and the growler, I got a mini workout in. Thank goodness this place has an elevator, or you'd have had to rescue me from the stairwell."

Lucas laughed as he carried the growler to the kitchen. "You want some of this now?"

I shook my head, wandering around the large living room as he stepped out of sight. "I'll get something at dinner."

"I think we have just enough time for a tour before we go," he said, closing the fridge. He spread his arms out as he rounded the marble-topped island and rejoined me in the living room. "First impressions? Besides the view. What do you think of the place?"

"I think it's—"

Before I could answer, a trio of voices somewhere over my left shoulder all burst in with their opinions and I cringed.

"I think it's wonderful!" Gwen gushed, floating a couple feet off the floor. "Scarlet, did you see the *two* sinks in the bathroom? You could move right in!"

"It's all fun and games until the elevator goes out and you're stuck walking up fourteen flights of stairs,"

Flapjack, my deceased Himalayan cat added. "Not to mention the musty smell in the closet. I think someone must have kept a dead body in there. Or, maybe it's *still* there, you know, behind the drywall!"

"Ew, Flapjack!" Gwen snapped. "Don't be morbid!"

"Quite distasteful, Flapjack," Hayward Kensington III chimed in. His Oxford accent emphasized his distaste of the grumpy cat's commentary.

Across the living room, Lucas's smile faltered. "Is it that bad? I mean, it's a little cold. And the art isn't really my taste, but—"

I laughed and took a step toward him. "No, no, it's not the art. I like it."

"Then why the hesitation—" He paused, one brow lifted. "They're here, aren't they?"

My nose wrinkled. "Maaaaybe?"

"Scar …" He threw his head back, pleading with the ceiling.

"I thought we'd marked this as a one-on-one kind of thing," he said, then glanced past me and quickly added, "No offense to any of you, of course."

Flapjack scoffed. "The only thing I find offensive is the amount of hair products he keeps in that musty bathroom."

Gwen giggled. "He clearly knows what he's doing with all of it. Though I'd be willing to bet he looks just as good first thing in the morning. Tousled hair, pajama bottoms … no shirt—"

Beside her, Hayward cleared his throat. Loudly.

I sighed. "They wanted to come see the city and so, I kinda offered to let them tag along," I said, ignoring the paranormal peanut gallery. "They're not staying! I promise."

Swiveling around, I shot Flapjack a meaningful glance. "In fact … I think they were just leaving, now that they've seen the place."

"Mhmm." Lucas didn't look convinced.

I made an overly dramatic *shoo'ing* gesture at the ghostly trio. "Go on. See the sights, breathe in the smells."

"Pike's Market, here I come!" Flapjack said with glee. "That's where they throw the fish," he informed Hayward and Gwen.

I cringed. The fish market was likely already closed, but I wasn't going to be the one to tell him.

"We should be taking our leave as well," Hayward said, holding his arm out for Gwen. "We're having dinner aboard a cruise ship this evening."

"And by *having dinner* he means watching other people eat while eavesdropping on their conversations," Gwen explained in a conspiratorially whisper, as if Lucas might overhear her. Which, strictly speaking, wasn't possible.

"Enjoy! See you in the morning. Not a minute before ten-thirty!" I called after the three ghosts as they floated back out the front door. "I'm putting up a salt ring, just in case."

"You'd think a simple Do Not Disturb sign would do the trick," Lucas said, coming to join me.

"Oh, to live in such a world," I said, laughing.

He kissed me and I tasted the craft beer on his lips. "Someone had a sample," I teased when we broke apart. "Did I get the right one?"

"It's perfect. Thank you." He smiled. "Why does it feel like longer than three weeks since the last time I saw you?"

"I was thinking the same thing during the drive," I confessed. "New Orleans seems like it was a year ago, not a month."

Lucas glanced down at the floor between us for a moment before meeting my eyes again. "How are you doing with everything?"

He wasn't talking about business at my flower shop or life with my pack of ghosts. There was a deeper specificity to his question. One I wasn't interested in discussing. At least, not tonight.

I smiled. "Things are good. I should have given you a head's up about the gang tagging along. I guess I was kind of hoping they'd take a hint and slip out mid-tour."

Lucas furrowed his brows as a slow smile tugged at his lips. "Really, Scar? I might not be able to hear them, but even *I* know there's no way they'd leave voluntarily."

I cringed. He was right, of course. The trio wasn't exactly known for being respectful of our privacy.

Now, with Lucas permanently stationed in Seattle, we'd need to establish some ground rules. Whether the ghosts agreed to them or not was a separate battle.

"It's been hard for me to say no to them since we got back from New Orleans," I told him. "I guess I still feel a little guilty over the way I treated them before leaving for the trip, especially when we both would have been in real trouble had they not come to the rescue."

Lucas gave an understanding smile and brushed a loose strand of my copper-colored hair out of my face. "Fair enough. I'd probably still be sitting in a jail cell if it hadn't been for them, and you."

"And now look at you," I said, gesturing at the large living space. "Living like a king!"

He laughed and captured one of my hands. "You should see my new office. Maybe next visit, you can meet me there."

"Deal. Now, let's talk about these dinner reservations you made. How fancy do I need to get?"

We were celebrating, his new job, his new condo, and his permanent move to Seattle. He'd made reservations as soon as he'd moved in and received his hire-on bonus with the international security firm. I wasn't sure of the dollar amount, but judging on the rental they'd put him up in, the company wasn't hurting for cash and was generous to its employees.

Forty-five minutes later, I was sufficiently dressed up enough to fit the dress code standards of the high-end restaurant Lucas had selected. He wore a three-piece suit—and looked darn good doing it—and as we walked to our table, I noticed more than a few pairs of female eyes turn toward him. I smiled to myself, thinking of Gwen's reaction if she'd stuck around long enough to see us leave for dinner.

We were seated and within a few minutes, we'd ordered a bottle of wine and a round of appetizers.

The prices on the menu made my eyes bug out, but I held my tongue. It was Lucas's night and this was how he wanted to celebrate. I'd grown up with money; extravagant dinners were nothing new to me. I had a handle on which fork to use for which course and knew the difference between a palate-cleansing sorbet and a true dessert by the time I was four. But I'd left that life behind—much to my parents' chagrin—and rarely dipped a toe in the 24-karat-gold swimming pool of the rich and famous.

As we waited for our entrees, we nibbled on fondue and considered the interior of the restaurant. It was a beautiful building and everything from the linens to the art to the furnishings had been carefully selected to create an elegant, almost old-world atmosphere.

"So, you've told me the office is cool. What about the people? Your team?" I asked, pouring myself a little more wine.

"It's different," he said, giving a nod when I hovered the bottle over the rim of his glass. "I'm not used to working in an office or keeping regular hours. It's a lot of meetings and collaboration, which is nice, but I'm adjusting to not being the lead." He chuckled. "That sounded more arrogant than I intended."

I shook my head and set the wine aside after topping off Lucas's glass. "I don't think it's arrogance. You're used to boots on the ground, giving the orders, and keeping everyone on track. Sitting in a boardroom making plans for things happening half a world away is a huge shift."

He raised his glass. "It is."

"You'll adjust," I told him, smiling over the rim of my own glass. "I have no doubt."

"Well, I'll get my first taste of field work here in a few weeks."

My eyebrows lifted.

"I've received my first international assignment," he said. "To Spain. I'll be gone for three weeks."

My heart sank. I'd known travel was part of the job requirements, but hadn't expected it to come so soon or to last for so long. We'd spent our entire relationship living long-distance. He'd spent more time in Beechwood Harbor with me, but only for a few weeks here and there in between filming assignments for the reality TV show he'd worked on.

I couldn't say why this new development was different than the past, but it tugged on some new thread of emotion and I had to work to force a smile. "That sounds exciting! Spain is lovely."

He went into some of the details and I did my best

to listen and keep my smile in place, but something a few tables down drew my attention away. A ghost was hovering over a diner, a malicious gleam in her haunted eyes. The ghost, a female who looked to have passed away while still in her teen years, dipped her silvery, semi-transparent hands into the middle-aged woman who was enjoying a chocolate tart. The woman sat up a little, her shoulders lifted.

The teenage ghost cackled and touched the woman again.

My eyes narrowed.

"Scarlet?" Lucas said, concern in his voice. "Is something wrong?"

"I—I'm sorry," I said, tearing my attention away from the ghosts. "I thought I saw someone I went to school with. But I was wrong." I reached for my wine glass. "You were saying?"

"Um, just that I'm looking forward to—"

I signaled for a passing server.

"Scarlet, what is going on?" Lucas asked, leaning forward.

"I'm sorry. It's just, there's something of a situation over there at that table—"

The server stopped at the table and I asked for a salt shaker. They weren't readily available on the table and my small clutch wasn't large enough for the small iron omelette pan I usually carted around in case of ghost misbehavior. The server masked a strange look and hurried off to find me one.

"What are you going to do with a salt shaker?" Lucas asked.

"Scare off that ghost over there before it goes any further. I don't know if they know how to possess someone, but if they don't already, they're about three seconds away from figuring it out."

The server was nowhere to be seen, and the ghost was dipping her hands back into the woman. I jolted to my feet. Lucas swore quietly. I marched across the dining room, eyes boring into the teenager's silver-hued profile. I cleared my throat and the two diners as well as the ghost turned to look at me.

The teenage ghost reared back as she met my eyes and realized I was glaring at her instead of blankly looking past her.

"Can we help you?" the man asked, giving me a suspicious frown.

I narrowed my eyes at the ghost before rearranging my face into a polite smile for the man and his wife. "I'm terribly sorry to interrupt. I thought you looked familiar, but it appears I was mistaken. Enjoy your meal."

"Oh, um, well, thank you?" the man said.

I turned and stalked back to my table with Lucas.

"You can see me?" The ghost hissed, right on my heels. "How? Who are you? What's your name?"

I ignored the ghost's questions, happy to have distracted her from the unsuspecting couple in time. The server reappeared at the table and held out a silver salt shaker. I quickly took it and gripped it in one hand, concealing it from the ghost behind me.

"Is there anything else, ma'am?" the server asked, a wariness in her eyes. "Your entrees should be here shortly."

"Thank you, this should do it," I told her, retaking my seat calmly.

The teen swooped closer. "Hey! I'm talking to you! What are you? How can you see me?"

Under the table, I shook salt into my open palm, collecting a small pile as quickly as possible.

When I didn't answer, the ghost shifted her attention to Lucas. "Hmm. He's yummy." She reached for his hand resting on the table. "I wonder what it would feel like to touch him."

"Leave us alone!" I hissed, hurling the salt in the ghost's face.

She shrieked and then growled before dispersing into a cloud of silver that faded away like an early morning cloud.

Lucas blinked. "Scarlet!"

"Sorry," I said, setting the salt shaker aside. "Just doing a little pest control."

He glanced around.

"It's all clear. Problem solved," I said, brushing my hands together to rid them of the excess salt. "Now, have I ever told you about the cafe I waitressed at in Barcelona?"

CHAPTER 2

"Lizzie, can you get me the bucket of pink carnations from the cooler?"

"Sure!" my assistant chirped from the front of the flower shop.

Moments later, the cheerful blonde appeared at my side and placed a five-gallon bucket of cherry-blossom pink flowers at my feet. "This looks great, so far!" she said, studying the large funeral wreath I was crafting.

"Thanks," I said, tucking another piece of boxwood into the squishy block of floral foam that formed the ring. With a quick sideways glance, I plucked a full carnation from the bucket, placed it in the arrangement, and then glanced up to identify the other sparse spots. "I should have finished it yesterday."

"It's all right," Lizzie said. "You're almost done and the service is still a few hours away. Plenty of time."

Lizzie's boundless optimism was one of the qualities I'd grown to love over the past several months since hiring her on as a part-time assistant at my flower shop, Lily Pond. When she'd started, she hadn't known the difference between a peony and a petunia, but she'd proved to be a quick study and was capable of most basic design orders on her own. Her early klutzy streak was fading, replaced with an ever-growing confidence in her skills since I'd hired her on full-time.

During my time visiting Lucas in New Orleans, I'd had my reservations about leaving the shop in her hands, but found things in perfect order and even received a handful of phone calls from our regular customers to let me know they appreciated her service in my absence.

I paused to tuck a stray strand of hair behind my ear and glanced at the white board calendar on the wall behind Lizzie. She side-stepped out of my way and gestured at the colorful writing. "These are the only ones left for today. I can finish up while you run this over to the funeral home. We've been pretty dead up front most of the day. I think a lot of people are down at the beach for the cleanup."

"Oh, you're probably right! I hadn't even thought about that." I blew out a puff of air. "Sheesh, this day is getting away from me."

The kids were back in school and tourist season—along with wedding season—was officially done for another year. To celebrate another successful busy season, the town's chamber of commerce had pulled together a potluck-style barbecue on the beach (weather permitting) and had invited all local vendors and their families to come celebrate. Taking advantage of the gathering, the mayor decided to host an all-day town beautification event preceding it. Tourist season was great for the town's businesses, but wreaked havoc on the beach and streets as people poured into town. Beechwood Harbor was a small town but a popular stop for fellow Washingtonians as well as people from all across the country. Some of whom were not as eco-minded as others. To counteract the damage, city council arranged discount booklets featuring coupons to local companies to be handed out to those participating in the cleanup projects all around town and down on the beach itself.

I'd donated several hanging baskets to one of the local clubs and had struck a deal with a local nursery to deliver a truckload of leftover annuals directly to the town's senior center. The mayor gifted me a coupon book in exchange for my help, assuaging my guilt over not being available to comb the beach for trash on the final day of the town beautification.

"Are you going to the barbecue tonight?" Lizzie asked.

I nodded and placed a few more carnations. "I was planning on swinging by. You?"

She hesitated and I glanced up. Lizzie's cheeks had gone pink and she was chewing her lower lip. "I'm not sure."

"Oh, come on. It'll be fun! You play a little beach volleyball. Dance. Mingle. Have some spiked punch."

Flapjack chuckled from his place on my work table. "As I recall, Scar, the last time you went to a barbecue, you didn't do any of that. You stuffed yourself with an impressive amount of potato salad, fell asleep on a picnic blanket, and woke up with a nasty sun burn."

I scowled at him. "Mrs. Garland makes prize-worthy potato salad and you're just jealous you can't have any!"

Realizing I'd said the quiet part out loud, I winced and peeked over at Lizzie. "I mean, you'd be *jealous* if you didn't get any. So you might want to get there early!"

"Nice save," Flapjack purred, his wheezy version of a laugh catching in his throat.

"Well, actually, someone asked me to go to the barbecue, but I'm not sure if it's a date or if it's just an *as friends* kind of thing." Lizzie paused, wringing her hands together. "So, I wasn't sure I'd go at all. The whole thing is making me nervous."

I smiled, resisting the urge to pounce on her. "Who asked you?"

Lizzie had been woefully single since I'd met her, and while we'd never talked too much about her past, I'd gathered a fair dose of heartbreak resided somewhere in the not-too-distant rear view.

Hayward, who'd been hanging out in the shop most of the day, shifted uncomfortably and rose from his seat. "Come along, Flapjack. I believe I know girl talk when I hear it. Perhaps we gentlemen should scurry along."

"Scurry along?" Flapjack snorted. "That's rich, coming from the guy who reads *Cosmo* over Lizzie's shoulder."

Hayward bristled, his bristle-brush mustache twitching. "That's preposterous!"

Flapjack smiled like the Cheshire.

"In any case"—Hayward bumped him with a quick elbow—"we should go. Gwen will be at the beach by now, waiting for us to join her."

"Fine." Flapjack glared up at Hayward but got to his feet, his feather-duster tail swirling like a boat propeller. "I was going anyway," he said casually. "They'll start grilling the fish soon."

With that, he winked out of sight, off to wander the beach and breathe in the scent of the fresh-caught fish. A ghost's life didn't usually have many pleasures. Flapjacks revolved around sarcasm and the smell of fish.

Hayward righted his top hat and vanished.

"Do you know Bryant Lewis?" Lizzie asked, drawing my attention back to her date-or-not-a-date quandary. "He's a checker over at Hank's Hardware."

"Oh, a *checker*, there's a stable future," Flapjacks disembodied voice called.

I bit down on the insides of my cheeks to keep from barking his name.

I'd make the little fur ball pay later. He was lucky Lizzie couldn't hear him.

"I think I've talked to him before," I said. "Sandy brown hair, looks like he played football in high school?"

Lizzie blushed. Clearly she'd admired his squared shoulders a time or two.

I smiled. "You should go. Even if it's not a date, you'll have a good time and make all the other single ladies jealous." I winked and brushed my hands off on my apron. A month had passed since my last manicure, though I'd never gotten around to fully taking off the remaining polish. I silently noted it was time for a return to the town's day spa and wondered if there was a coupon in the booklet from the mayor.

Now that I'd be seeing Lucas a lot more often, I needed to start scheduling regular manicures. Not for him, per say. Lucas might wear a suit for his new job and live in a fancy high-rise, but at heart, he was a jeans-and-t-shirt kind of guy, he drove a truck, hated frou-frou coffee, and probably hadn't even noticed the manicure I'd had done before visiting him in the Big Easy. Despite his no-frills preference, there were bound to be company parties, corporate functions, and dinner parties in our future as he settled into his new job. Green nails and tattered cuticles simply wouldn't do.

I should probably get a few more dresses and purses too...

Gwen would be delighted to help. She inhaled fashion magazines like oxygen and spent the majority of her time haunting—literally—the town beauty parlor. If I told her I needed a wardrobe update, she'd no doubt have ten suggestions at the tips of her fingers.

"All right," I said, carefully lifting the large—and heavy—arrangement from my workstation. "I'm going to take everything over to the funeral home. If it's still dead once you've finished those last few orders, go ahead and lock up early and head to the barbecue. I'll see you, and *Bryant*, down there."

Lizzie flushed again and scurried to prop open the back door for me.

Within ten minutes, I had the arrangements loaded into the Lily Pond delivery van and was backing out of the shop's designated parking space. Beechwood Harbor was a small town, the kind of place where the shops were named after their owner or their owner's parents who'd originally opened the place. There was one market, one coffee house, a handful of restaurants, and a few motels and bed-and-breakfasts. I drove down Main Street through town and within minutes, pulled into the small lot beside the funeral home.

As the town's sole flower shop, Lily Pond did a lot of business with the funeral home and no one was surprised to see me when I backed through the glass side door, arms wrapped around a large hurricane vase. The flowers obscured my face, but a passing employee greeted me by name all the same.

"Need some help?" Garth asked, after we exchanged pleasantries.

"Maybe with the wreath. I'll be right back up for it."

"Sure thing, Scarlet."

"Thanks!"

I knew the place like the back of my hand—not hard to do, considering its size—and quickly made my way to the small viewing room where memorial services were often held. There were two churches in town, but the smaller or non-religious services tended to be held right at the funeral home. It was one of the town's historic homes that now housed small businesses. In the funeral home's case, almost everything in the interior remained original to the home, with only some minor updating to modern codes.

Services were held in the former living room, a large space with polished wood floors, a large fireplace, and built-in shelving along one wall. It was always set up and ready for a service, with rows of folding wooden chairs, a thick carpet down the aisle, a pulpit at the front that blocked part of the fireplace from view, and a few tables for flowers. The service tonight was a memorial service and wouldn't have a casket, so I'd designed a large wreath of flowers that would hang from an easel beside a blown-up portrait of the deceased.

The large hurricane vase in my arms went on the table beside the urn, just as I'd discussed with the family when they'd come for their consultation. The funeral home had several package options available for those who didn't want one more decision to make, but oftentimes families wanted to meet with me and discuss the arrangements ahead of time. The woman being memorialized the following day had been young at the time of her death, only forty-six. She'd left behind both her parents along with a brother, and, perhaps most tragically, a teenage daughter.

The arrangement shifted slightly and I paused to maneuver some of the blooms back into their rightful places.

"This is all for me?"

I turned, startled by the voice, and found a ghost standing in the doorway of the viewing room, her mouth agape, silvery eyes wide.

Crap. Had she seen me? Did she know I'd heard her?

Without a word, I did a dramatic stretch, pressing my palms into my sides and arching backward, trying to convince the ghost I'd had some kind of muscle spasm.

What can I say, desperate times, pathetic measures.

The ghost watched me, but I avoided meeting her gaze head-on and went back to arranging the flowers. If she didn't know I'd heard her, then she wouldn't know I could see her, and she'd leave me alone.

And, above all, I could make it to the barbecue before all of Mrs. Garland's potato salad was gone.

CHAPTER 3

The spirit came further into the viewing room, her limbs awkward. Perfect. Not only is there a ghost wandering around, but it's a helpless baby ghost. *Ugh. Why me?*

It usually takes new ghosts a little while to get the hang of their new mode of transportation. While they no longer require the use of their legs to get from point A to point B, most try to keep using their legs anyway. Muscle memory is a hard thing to break, even after death.

I glanced at the large portrait at the front of the room and then back at the ghost. It was Sabrina Hutchins, the woman being memorialized. Before I could decide whether or not to blow my cover—and possibly my chance at a plateful of potato salad—the air beside Sabrina shimmered and a second spirit appeared. This one wearing feather earrings and a wide smile as she waved at me. "Scarlet! There you are!"

I cringed and looked away.

"Oh, excuse me. Am I interrupting something?" Gwen said, presumably to Sabrina. "I don't think we've met before. I'm Gwen."

"Sabrina," the second ghost said.

I fussed with a pair of roses, wishing ghost telepathy came along with all my other whackadoodle gifts.

"Yoohoo! Scarlet!" Gwen called.

"You know she can't see you, right? I'm new to this, but it's pretty obvious we're ghosts and the living can't see or hear us."

Gwen laughed. "Scarlet's not like most—"

Crap.

I shoved a rose back into place and spun on my heels to face both spirits, shooting daggers at Gwen.

Sabrina blinked. "You can *see* me?"

Crossing my arms, I nodded. "Yes, and I'm sorry, but I'm really busy and I don't have a lot of time for small talk."

Sabrina didn't look offended. She propelled herself to the altar, her gaze fixed on the large portrait of herself.

"Oh, honey. Is this *your* service?" Gwen asked her, floating a few paces behind. "You're a new ghost?"

Sabrina nodded.

Gwen shot me a look. "Scar, we have to help her."

"Help me how?" Sabrina asked. "I'm already dead. Seems a little late to do much of anything. I can't hop back in my body and force myself to wake up from this nightmare." She peeked at Gwen. "Can I?"

Gwen gave a solemn shake of her head. "No. I'm afraid what's done is done. Do you know how you died?"

"Not really." Sabrina paused, staring at the urn. "Is that—um—*me*?"

Gwen looked at me and I nodded. With that confirmation, the 70s-era spirit sidled up to Sabrina and placed a steadying hand at her back. "It is," she said softly. "It looks like your family had your remains cremated."

A sob caught in Sabrina's throat and Gwen moved closer, pulling the woman into an embrace. "It's okay. We'll help you adjust to your new life. It's cliché, but really, it does help to think of this as a new beginning rather than an ending."

I poked my head out into the hallway, making sure no one was within earshot. The funeral home didn't boast a large staff, but with a service hours away from beginning, the funeral home director, Karla Leeson, and her two staff members were bound to be nearby finishing the preparations. Communicating with ghosts was a gift, but it came with a whole host of complications. Mostly that by and large, people would think I was certifiable if I told them the truth. I had a handful of tricks to get away with public ghost chats, the most popular of which was a small Bluetooth earpiece I could use to make it appear as though I were talking to someone on the phone rather than to thin air.

The earpiece was back at the flower shop, and therefore not an option for the current conversation. Gwen knew I didn't like chatting with strange ghosts outside my set aside office hours, but she had a heart of gold and wasn't likely to enforce the rules when presented with a newcomer who needed assistance.

"Gwen," I said, jerking my head to beckon her closer, "a word."

Reluctantly, Gwen disentangled herself from Sabrina and floated across the viewing room to join me. "Scarlet! I can't believe you were just pretending you couldn't see or hear her!"

Guilt nipped at me but I did my best to ignore it. "Her service is starting in two hours. I don't really think it's a good idea for her to be here."

"Why not?"

"She's not going to feel better if she sits and listens to her family and friends eulogize her and then watch them all go back to their normal lives while she has to stay behind. That can't possibly be helpful."

"You never know. It might be." Gwen paused and glanced at Sabrina's back. "I guess I could take her down to the barbecue. I could introduce her around, show her that there's plenty of fun to be had in the afterlife!"

I chewed my lower lip. "I don't know. That might be too much."

The full force of Beechwood Harbor's ghost brigade was overwhelming to me, and I saw a good majority of them on a daily basis.

"Well, what do you suggest?" Gwen asked, tossing her hands up. "No funeral and no barbecue, so what? I could take her to Siren's Song and let her decompress."

"The coffee shop? How would that help?"

"I don't know," she shrugged. "The espresso machine is like white noise."

Of my three permanent ghostly companions, Gwen was not the one I'd choose for new-ghost orientation. She was a vivacious spirit with a fuller afterlife than most of the living enjoyed while still breathing. She also had a tendency to talk a hundred miles an hour and forget that not everyone wants to be the life of the party.

Why couldn't Flapjack have been the one to come find me? He wouldn't have given Sabrina more than a second glance.

Which reminded me ...

"What are you even doing here?" I asked Gwen. "I thought you were down at the beach already. Flapjack and Hayward left a while ago to go meet you."

"Oh!" Gwen's eyes brightened. "Well, I *was* at the beach and you're never going to believe what I just heard!"

I groaned. "You came all this way to gossip?"

BIG GHOSTS DON'T CRY

Gwen blinked. "Of course!"

Sabrina turned. "What am I supposed to do, now? Why am I even here?"

Torn between a ghost's existential crisis and Gwen's gossip-fest. Lucky me.

"Usually, it means you have some kind of unfinished business. Any idea what that might be?" Gwen asked, her tone of voice overly cheery, as if asking the woman if she'd seen the most recent Nicolas Sparks movie.

"I—I don't know," Sabrina replied. "I don't even know what happened to me! How did I die?"

Gwen looked at me expectantly.

"I—I don't know," I said. "I'm just here to deliver the flowers." I gestured at the nearest bouquet.

"Who ordered them?" Sabrina asked, gliding a little more gracefully toward the wreath at the front of the room. "My parents?"

"Yes," I replied softly. "They picked out everything personally. They told me lilacs were your favorites. We used lavender here."

"It's pretty. Thank you."

Gwen gave me a pained look. "Maybe you could do the ... *thing*?"

My eyes widened, shocked she'd even bring it up.

"What thing?" Sabrina asked. "Please, if there's anything you can do to help me--"

"I have a support group for ghosts," I told her, giving Gwen a warning glance. "Local ghosts come to my flower shop once a week to talk about their experiences and offer each other help and support. There are ghosts in every stage of, er, afterlife. It might help."

"I'll be there, too," Gwen offered helpfully. "Do you want me to come and get you? Will you be here, you think?" She glanced around the viewing room with a wary eye.

"I—I don't know. I guess so." She shrugged and glanced around the room. "I haven't tried leaving yet."

"Wait, you woke up here?" I asked.

Sabrina nodded.

That was a little odd. In my experience, ghosts usually started their new life at the place their previous one had ended. So, unless Sabrina kicked it at the funeral home, she was a little delayed. Her earthly life had ended a week and a half ago, according to the information I'd gathered from her parents. They'd pushed things out to make the arrangements for the service and to allow time for her extended family to make travel plans, as most of them lived out of state.

I glanced at my watch. The barbecue was starting in fifteen minutes. Everyone would be trekking down to the sand carrying coolers, beach chairs, and picnic blankets. The kids would have all their sandcastle-making tools, and there were bound to be at least a dozen dogs running around, barking at seagulls. I'd told Lizzie I would meet her down there.

Then there was the potato salad. And yes, it really was *that* good.

"I have to get going," I said, a new flurry of impatience welling up. "I have to go home and change and get my strawberry pie from the fridge. Listen, Sabrina, come to the support group. We'll talk more then, okay?"

The woman nodded but I couldn't decide whether she intended to follow through or not. Gwen glanced at me. There was no doubt she was itching to get back to the beach. When the whole town gathered, there was bound to be gossip buzzing like a hive of bees, and Gwen would be there to scoop up as much honey as she could. As much as she wanted to help Sabrina, she wouldn't be able to resist the call back to the beach.

"Are you sure you want to stay here?" she asked gently. "The barbecue will be a lot more fun."

"I'll be fine," Sabrina said, her jawline set.

Gwen looked at me. I shrugged.

"Okay. Well, if you change your mind, you know where to find us."

I left the viewing room with Gwen in tow. Karla came around the corner, clipboard in hand, and offered me a warm smile. Garth, her full-time employee, followed right behind, carefully carrying the large wreath of flowers.

"Thank you, Garth. I got the easel all prepped," I told him.

He nodded and then continued into the viewing room.

Karla smiled. "Beautiful work, as always."

"Thank you."

"Are you heading to the barbecue?" she asked.

"After a quick pit stop back home," I replied with a nod.

"Maybe I'll see you later then," Karla replied. She gestured at the doors of the viewing room. "It's a small affair tonight. I don't imagine the service will take long and they've opted to have the reception offsite."

Smiling, I raised a hand and moved to sidestep her. "See you down there, then."

As soon as I started the delivery van's engine, Gwen winked into the passenger seat and started babbling about Lizzie's maybe-date with Bryant from the hardware store. "According to Tanya, Bryant just got out of a two year long-distance relationship with his high school sweetheart. He's not exactly on the rebound, but he hasn't been single long. Although, with those shoulders and that chin dimple—"

"Gwen!" I snapped.

She jolted, her eyes going wide. "What?"

"Why did you tell that woman I could help her? And then to even *suggest* that I use my power on her! What were you thinking?"

"Oh. Well, I don't know, Scarlet. She seemed so sad, I thought maybe you could just … give her a little nudge."

I closed my eyes, silently counting to five when I stopped at the four-way intersection. When I opened them again, I smashed the heel of my hand against the turn signal and pulled the van to the left. "First of all, don't make it sound like it's not a big deal. It is and we both know it. I don't have a handle on my powers. For all I know, I could try to help her cross over and end up sling-shotting her to who knows where! I know you were only trying to help, but I'm not comfortable discussing my powers. Especially not with strange ghosts."

"I'm sorry, Scarlet." Gwen's eyes dropped to the floor between us. "I wasn't trying to cause problems."

"I know," I said gently, wishing I could reach out and pat her arm for reassurance. I hadn't meant to snap at her, but I needed to get the point across, and sometimes Gwen wasn't the best at picking up subtleties.

I drew in a deep breath and smiled at her. "It's all right. No harm done. And I think after some time to think, Sabrina will join our group. Can you try to swing by and invite her again, once it's closer to Tuesday's meeting, I mean?"

That made her brighten. Gwen was frozen in time right at her peak, barely out of her teen years when she took an ill-fated header off a stage at an outdoor music festival. Her feathered hair was silver hued, along with the rest of her, but I knew that if I'd met her in life, I'd have mistaken her for a young Farah Fawcett from that iconic red bathing suit shot. She had an open face with expressive eyes and an easy smile. With Gwen, I never had to wonder what she was thinking. One, because she was a total chatterbox and always said exactly what was on her mind, and two, because the girl had zero chance of ever developing a poker face.

Gwen had no desire to leave her spectral life. She loved being a ghost and spent her days as the maven of Beechwood Harbor's spirit community. Since I'd moved to town, she'd latched onto me as a conduit to help her many friends and was nearly single-handedly responsible for the weekly meetings I held to help local ghosts. In exchange, she made sure—well, she did her best—to keep ghosts from interrupting me or approaching me cold on the street….

Or while at the grocery store. Or visiting the local coffee house. Or dining at a restaurant. Or, and perhaps most importantly, whilst driving.

Not to mention, Hayward had a massive crush on her, and I was fairly certain those feelings were reciprocated. They'd gone back and forth a little in recent weeks, but at my last inquiry, they were inching ever nearer to making things official. Though, I wasn't 100% sure what that entailed, considering they were both dead. I'd never asked, unsure I ever wanted to find out what went on behind the closed doors of a spirit-world boudoir.

I pulled the van into its designated spot and cut the engine.

"Go on ahead," I told Gwen. "I'm going to go upstairs and change. I'll meet you down at the beach. Try to scare off anyone by the potato salad."

She laughed and then made a mock salute. "You got it! Bye, Scar!"

With a swirl, she zoomed out the side of the van door.

※ ※ ※ ※ ※ ※ ※ ※

FIFTEEN MINUTES LATER, my toes were buried in the sand and a plate of Mrs. Garland's potato salad balanced on my knees. I'd changed into a pair of denim shorts and a black tank top. I wore a floppy sunhat to keep my fair skin away from the sun's harsh rays, all the while hoping for a tiny bit of color on my stems.

The beach was packed with locals. Most congregated around the two folding tables laden down with the potluck dishes. A volleyball net was set up closer to the surf and currently hosted a three-on-three of high school teens. The boys had stripped their t-shirts off and the girls were trying—and failing miserably—not to ogle.

"Ah, young love."

I snorted at Flapjack's sudden appearance in the beach chair beside me. "I think you've got the wrong L-word, my friend. After all, no one does desperate lust quite like a pack of teenagers."

Flapjack smiled. "I miss those days. Back when you

kissed a Justin Timberlake poster every night before bed."

"I did not!" I protested, even as my cheeks warmed, no doubt a tomato red that I couldn't blame on the late afternoon sun.

"Scar, that thing had enough lip gloss kiss prints, it could have doubled as a *Revlon* ad."

"Gee, how lucky I am to have a walking, talking time capsule," I muttered, sinking down in my chair. I shoveled in a bite of potato salad, the tangy bliss perking up my mood.

Flapjack swished his tail, clearly pleased with himself. "I'll always be here to remind you of your glory days."

"Wonderful."

I shoved another bite of potato salad into my mouth and swallowed hard when a shadow appeared in the sand beside my own. "This seat taken?"

I craned around and saw Chief Jeffery Lincoln standing behind Flapjack's chair. "No, please, sit."

Flapjack shot me a dirty look and jumped down a moment before Chief sat on—or, rather, *through*—him. He hiked his tail in the air and started down the beach. A few other ghosts dotted the party, invisible guests to the afternoon barbecue, some of whom had been in town since its founding. Across the way, chatting with Gwen and Hayward, were Posy and Earl, the town's original founders.

"Are you enjoying the barbecue?" Chief Lincoln

asked, stabbing his fork through a juicy piece of late-season watermelon.

"I am, thanks. And you?"

"Definitely. It's one of my favorite annual celebrations," he replied, bobbing his head. "It's nice when everyone gets together like this, and the beach cleanup was a big success."

"It does look great. And so much *quieter* now."

He chuckled. "I can't stay long, though."

"Oh?"

"There's a service up at the funeral home, and I'm making it a point to be there for the family."

"You mean Sabrina Hutchins' service?"

"That's right." He gave me a curious look.

"I just dropped off the flowers," I explained.

"Oh, right! Of course."

"Did you know her?" I asked, scooping up my next bite.

"Not personally. I'm part of the investigation, working with the Pine Shoals PD."

My spoon stilled midway to my mouth. "Investigation?"

Chief nodded. "Tragically, Sabrina was murdered."

A hot knife of guilt sliced through me and I put my fork down, my appetite gone.

CHAPTER 4

The festive barbecue faded to the background as Chief Lincoln's words sunk in, echoing through my mind. "Murdered?" I repeated, suddenly feeling too cold.

Chief Lincoln looked pained. "Sorry. I assumed you knew. It was in the paper."

"Oh, I don't usually get around to reading it," I said.

He rubbed a hand over the back of his neck. "She was attacked in her home. At this point, we think it might be a copycat to the Seaside Strangler."

Now *that* case I'd heard about. Two summers ago, before I'd even moved to Beechwood Harbor, a serial killer had moved up the coast, murdering three women and attempting a fourth, before he was apprehended. The case made national news and had caught my attention even while I'd been home with my family in Arizona.

"My mom tried to talk me out of moving here because of that case," I told Chief Lincoln. "If he hadn't been caught in the weeks before my move, I'm pretty sure she would have followed me to the airport and staged a sit-in, right there on the tarmac."

Chief smiled. "She sounds like my mother. During my first few weeks of police training, I was convinced she was going to pop out of the bushes and try to kidnap me."

I laughed softly. "I imagine you'd never have heard the end of that one, if she'd tried."

"No kidding!" He chuckled and popped the piece of watermelon into his mouth. "My grandmother calls me weekly to tell me that she has her whole church praying over me, and right before we hang up, she always reminds me to put the safety on my gun."

"That's adorable," I replied, grinning at him.

The darkness seeped away, and I put Sabrina in the back of my mind with a brief mental note to make sure Gwen looked after her.

"Are you here alone tonight?" Chief Lincoln asked, glancing around. "Where's Lucas? Holly mentioned he was moving to town."

"Oh, well, not quite." I tucked a strand of hair behind my ear. "He's in Seattle now. He got a job offer with an international security firm and they put him up in a fancy corporate rental until he finds a more permanent place."

"Aha. Well good for him! I'll bet you're glad he's closer."

I smiled. "Seattle's still a little far away for my taste, but I'm glad he's in one place, at least for the most part."

Chief took a bite and chewed it thoughtfully while watching the volleyball players for a moment before scanning the beach. He was clearly off duty, but even so, there was something about the set of his shoulders and keenness to his eyes that told me he wasn't fully relaxed. He paused, something catching his eye, and a smile spread across his lips.

I followed his line of sight and found his fiancée, Cassie Frank, standing at the buffet line chatting with Holly Boldt and Adam St. James.

It always entertained me to think about Beechwood's residents interacting with supernatural beings, completely clueless to the power and magic that pulsed just under the surface of the sleepy town. The Haven Council and Supernatural Protection Agency would never let supernaturals go public, but I sometimes liked to think about the looks on people's faces if they were to ever realize a witch had been serving up their coffee or the shaggy black dog that raided the town dumpsters, rummaging for food, was actually the town's heartthrob.

Cassie and Chief Lincoln were both human and blissfully unaware of the magic world they lived in.

"How are the wedding plans coming along?" I asked.

Chief shrugged, still smiling. "I told Cassie to tell me when and where. The rest is up to her unless she needs help."

I laughed. "Smart man."

Chief Lincoln's phone chirped, and he reached for the case he wore clipped to his belt to silence it. "That's my cue," he said, pushing to his feet. "Enjoy the rest of the barbecue, Scarlet."

"Thanks, Chief."

I waved and he set off, his stride as purposeful as possible in the deep sand.

"Who was murdered?" Flapjack asked, winking back into the chair.

I jolted. "Don't do that!"

"What?"

I narrowed my eyes at him. "We've discussed the blinking in and out thing."

He sighed. "You really do take all the fun out of the afterlife, you know."

I rolled my eyes and scooped up my final bite before the wind could kick up sand and ruin it.

"Seriously, though. Are you gearing up for another turn as the ginger Nancy Drew?"

Mouth full, I shot him a scowl.

Flapjack swished his tail. "Fine. I'll make Gwen tell me. You know she can't keep a secret to save her life.

Well," he smirked, his whiskers twitching, "guess it's a little late for that anyway."

I leaned over, tugged at the beach tote I'd brought with me, and grabbed a small silver mister bottle. With two pumps, a lemon-infused mist sailed in Flapjack's direction. In the blink of an eye, the Himalayan arched his back, hackles raised. He hissed at me and then vanished.

I'd pay for it later, but I smiled to myself and enjoyed the newfound silence. I slipped the spray bottle back into the bag and went back to eating.

For whatever reason, Flapjack abhorred the scent of lemon and would flee from it in any form. So, when he really got under my skin, I made it a point to use lemon-scented cleaners around the house. It guaranteed me a sarcasm-free afternoon and came with the side benefit of having a clean apartment. A few weeks ago, a woman had come into my shop pitching her essential oil company, and I'd purchased a few vials of lemon oil and the small mister bottle.

The trick had just lost its sneak attack effect, but I also knew that next time I'd only have to brandish the bottle to get the mouthy cat off my case.

Win-win.

And now, I could enjoy the barbecue and the sunset in peace.

TUESDAY'S GHOST meeting kicked off at seven o'clock once the shop was closed and Lizzie had punched out. I held the meetings in Lily Pond, mostly because I didn't like the idea of a horde of strange ghosts upstairs in my apartment. Besides Flapjack, Hayward, and Gwen, I preferred to keep my home as a sanctuary away from nosy ghosts. For the most part, the local ghosts respected my ground rules largely because they knew that if they strayed outside the boundaries I'd put in place, I wouldn't help them, no matter how much they begged and pleaded. If they wanted my attention, they had to attend the weekly meeting and make their petition that way.

Every now and again, a pushy ghost would come along and force me to put up precautionary measures inside my house, usually a ring of salt around the baseboards, windows and doors. Of course, Hayward and Flapjack didn't appreciate being effectively locked out of their home, but they kept their grumbling to a minimum until a solution could be reached.

Gwen didn't stay at my apartment with us. She had enough haunts that she never slowed down long enough to ghost-sleep. Even when most of the town's residents were asleep, she'd be out exchanging information and gossip with other ghosts. I had no idea how they found enough to talk about. Beechwood Harbor wasn't a hip and happening hotspot. Beyond the occasional cheating spouse or new love affair, what could there be to talk about?

"I just wish I could get the hang of it," Loretta, a ghost in her mid-sixties, complained after listening to one of the new members talk about learning to channel energy into making things move. "All I want is to read a book again without having to hover over some patron's shoulder. It's so maddening waiting for them to catch up with me and turn the blasted page!"

Loretta had been a librarian in life and haunted the town library, fretting over the way her replacement stacked books and bemoaning the squeaky wheel on the metal cart. I had no proof, but I firmly believed that if she stepped away from the library, she'd find peace and be able to cross over into the Otherworld. Her desire to control every minute detail of the goings-on in her library was the tether keeping her here on this plane.

So far, she hadn't made it a day without darkening their door.

As the regular's discussed the benefits of being able to move small objects, I moved around the shop, dusting and polishing. I preferred to use the meetings as a time to catch up on the tasks that easily slipped through the cracks, especially over the weekend, which tended to be busy. I usually took Sunday and Monday off and kept the shop closed altogether on Monday so both Lizzie and I could have a dedicated day off each week. Though, with Lucas in Seattle, I was wondering if I should renegotiate the schedule with Lizzie and see about taking Saturday and Sunday off in order to have a proper weekend off. It was still early enough that Lucas didn't have his schedule down pat, so I was biding my time.

"Scarlet—"

I turned at Gwen's voice, feather duster stilled. "Hmm?"

She pointed at the door just as Sabrina slipped through the glass, a strange look on her face as though she still weren't entirely used to passing through solid materials. "Welcome, Sabrina," I greeted.

"I'm so glad you came!" Gwen said, surging forward to stand beside her. "Let me introduce you around."

Sabrina shied away before Gwen could reach her. Her silver eyes flashed as she looked at me. "It might have been nice if you'd told me what happened!"

I looked to Gwen but she looked caught off guard as well. "I—I'm sorry, but—"

"You played dumb, like you didn't know I'd been killed! Murdered in cold blood!"

The other ghosts in the circle collectively moved back, some sliding through the front display window and vanishing into the night. We'd had unstable ghosts before. It usually ended in a mess.

"Sabrina, I didn't know," I replied, lifting one hand

in surrender while the other slipped under the front counter and wrapped around the handle of the small omelette-sized cast iron pan I kept there for such occasions. Flapjack could be scared off with a splash of lemon, but other ghosts tended to need a little more convincing.

The business end of an iron pan did the trick.

"I only found out about the murder after I delivered the flowers. I swear."

I held the pan but kept it out of sight. I didn't want to use it on her. Though I wasn't entirely sure what the sensation was like, I had to assume it wasn't pleasant. But then, the last ghost that had gone berserk in my shop had blown out the glass on the front door and cost the landlord a pretty penny in the insurance deductible—a fact he reminded me of every time I dropped off my rent check.

Sabrina advanced on me, the light still blazing in her eyes. "I talked to some other ghosts around town and they told me about you."

Oh, brother. This ought to be good.

Hayward took a valiant step forward, arms outstretched as if to intercede. "Madame, this is—"

Sabrina ignored him, brushing right past him. "They said you can send me forward, into this … this *Otherworld*. Is that true?"

My fingers loosened their grip on the iron handle. "I've helped spirits cross over, but it's not some easy, flip-of-the-switch thing. I can't snap my fingers and send you off into the next realm."

"Then how does it work? How do I get out of this place?" The anger in her voice gave way to desperation. "I can't stay here another minute!"

"I'm not an expert," I started, my voice calm, "but like Gwen said at the funeral home, there's usually some sort of unfinished business keeping spirits here, in this realm, and the option to cross over only presents itself when that business is resolved. Now, seeing as you met death as the result of an act of violence, I'd guess that might be the thing holding you back. Do you have any idea who might have killed you? Any memory of that night at all?"

"No! I told you. I woke up in that funeral home. I don't know what happened to me." She began to tremble and her voice wavered. "Just—se—set me free—"

Without warning, she swelled and then dissolved into a cloud of silver-hued particles. The mist scattered through the room until it became invisible, like dust settling back to the ground. Only the echo of her voice lingered, the word *free* resounding through the air for an unnerving second before it was swallowed up in silence.

I blinked. "What just happened?"

Everyone started talking at once. The half dozen regulars, Gwen, and Hayward all offered up theories.

"She dispersed!" Gwen exclaimed.

"But *how?*" Loretta asked, staring at the place Sabrina had just stood. "There was no catalyst."

"Can one self-disperse?" Hayward asked, also studying the place on the floor.

I held up a hand. "Wait, if she dispersed, wouldn't she reboot back to where she first woke up as a ghost?"

"It's likely. Or, to a space she feels safe," Loretta replied.

"The funeral home?" Gwen suggested.

I glanced at the clock on the wall. It was after hours. No one would be at the funeral home to let us inside. Well, no one would be there to let *me* inside. Gwen and the others could charge in without hesitation.

"We'd better go check," I said, reaching for my keys.

THE FRONT ROOM of the funeral home was aglow when we arrived, Loretta, Gwen, and Hayward at my back. Flapjack preferred not to attend the weekly meetings, and the other attendees said goodbye as we left the flower shop.

"Someone's working late," Gwen said. "I'll bet it's Karla. Poor thing hasn't had a date in over a year."

I rolled my eyes. As someone who spent the majority of my life happily single, it grated when Gwen pitied the unattached as though they'd contracted an incurable disease.

"Who's going inside?" I asked the trio of ghosts.

"You're not coming with us, Lady Scarlet?" Hayward asked, concern etched in his distinguished face.

"I don't have a good reason to be here," I replied. "Karla will think it's weird if I knock on the front door without cause."

Hayward glanced up at the illuminated window. "Hmm. Perhaps you're right."

"Just go see if you can find Sabrina. If she wants to talk to me, I'll be out here."

Gwen looped her arm through Hayward's and gently tugged him into motion. "Come on."

Loretta hesitated. "I think I'll wait here, with Scarlet."

I glanced at her but didn't say anything.

Hayward and Gwen surged toward the doors and slipped inside the building. I stuffed my hands into the front pocket of my sweatshirt. The official beginning of autumn was still a few days away, but already the evenings had chilled dramatically from a week or two ago.

Loretta swayed in place beside me, a nervous energy radiating from her as she stared up at the historical home that had been converted to the town's funeral parlor somewhere along the way. "This is where my own memorial service was held," she said quietly. "It feels like only yesterday."

In reality, nearly twelve years had passed since Loretta's death. She'd been alone in the library, drinking tea while she worked through a stack of book returns from the busy day, when she'd suffered a stroke. When her part-timer came in the next morning, he'd found her and called the paramedics, but there was nothing that could be done. She'd already gone. Loretta, in her new form, had hovered nearby, watching the scene but powerless to say or do anything.

It was a tragic though not uncommon story. I'd heard variations of it dozens, perhaps hundreds, of times before.

"I'll bet it was a lovely service," I replied, giving her a small smile.

Loretta's strong type-A bent could be trying, but at heart she was a sweet woman and had been beloved by the entire town while she'd been alive.

She nodded. "It was. I remember being surprised at how many people attended. Some of them were children I'd read stories to on Saturday mornings, though now grown with children of their own."

"You've left a beautiful legacy," I said, wishing she'd find the strength to fully leave it behind. She wasn't happy and thriving as a spirit, like Gwen or Hayward. She spent her days wandering aimlessly, reminiscing about the past instead of looking to the future.

Suddenly, the urge to take her hand swelled up inside me. Logically, I knew that I couldn't *touch* her, though there'd been times where I felt almost able to reach out and stroke Flapjack's fur.

But that was because he'd been my cat in life. Wasn't it?

The urge thrummed through me, more urgently than before, and I reached for Loretta's hand. Our hands met, an electric shock radiating up my arm. Loretta looked up, her eyes round. "What are you—"

Before she could finish her sentence, her eyes fluttered closed and the sound of a long exhale filled my ears. I gripped her hand a little tighter and then released it. Loretta faded, her semi-transparent form breaking apart into a silver-purple mist. A bright light followed and I squinted against it. When my focus returned, I was alone on the sidewalk.

"Loretta?" I whispered, already knowing she couldn't answer.

She was gone.

Crossed over.

"Well, that was a bust."

I jumped at the sound of Gwen's voice and whipped around to find her and Hayward standing behind me.

"The young woman wasn't inside, as far as we could tell," Hayward added with an apologetic look.

"Where's Loretta?" Gwen asked.

Hayward heaved a sigh. "Back to her library, I imagine. You know how agitated she gets when she's been away for too long."

I stared, unblinking, at the place where she'd last stood, still not sure myself what had just happened.

"Scarlet? Are you all right?" Gwen asked, concern threading her voice as she swooped a little closer.

"She—she—I mean, I was standing here, she was there, and then, I *touched* her hand and she—*poof*."

"Lady Scarlet?" Hayward said, thick eyebrows raised. "What are you saying?"

"I—I just helped her cross over to the Otherworld."

CHAPTER 5

*L*oretta's crossing echoed through my memory on a loop as I tossed and turned in bed. It didn't make any sense. She wasn't the first ghost I'd witness cross over. Far from it. But she was the first one I'd actively participated in. In the past, I'd been a spectator. Why now?

Reaper.

I pressed my pillow against my ears, as if that could drown out the terrible word. It raked against my nerves and swirled my stomach in a way that made me feel out at sea on a less-than-seaworthy boat.

The word was still there, tumbling through my mind, accompanied by terrible Grim Reaper silhouettes accompanied by long scythes.

I am a Shepherd, I reminded myself, fighting against the shadows.

Loretta was ready to cross over. She'd been ready

since I'd met her, when Gwen corralled her into one of the first meetings we'd held at Lily Pond. Loretta had hated being a ghost. All she'd ever done was hang around the library, reading over people's shoulders and wringing her hands every time someone misplaced a book or dog-eared a page. She could spout off for a solid hour of the daily infractions, as if they were being presented before a judge and jury.

"He had the audacity to remove the dust jacket! A child in aisle ten was sneaking Doritos from the front pocket of a backpack and put his cheese dust-riddled fingers all over a first-edition Harry Potter hardback!"

On and on and on. And if I'd let her, she would have gone on like that for years. Decades, even! She was holding so tightly to her library that she would have lingered forever, waiting and watching, her anxiety and despair plaguing her until the end of time.

I'd done her a favor. She was at peace now.

I'd done my job.

That's what it was, after all. I was a Shepherd and I'd successfully herded Loretta into the Otherworld.

Then why did I feel so crappy about it?

"Ugh!" I flipped the covers off and flipped on the bedside lamp. My black Lily Pond sweatshirt lay discarded at the foot of the bed and I pulled it on. A pair of jeans and sneakers followed. I clicked off the light and tiptoed out into the hallway. According to the shiny tech watch Lucas had sent me a few weeks ago, it was 2:30 in the morning. Flapjack would be back from his gallivanting. Hayward tended to fall into a ghost sleep around midnight and would likely be snoring on the couch.

Silently, I moved into the main living area, a three-hundred square foot space comprised of a kitchen, dinette area, and a small living room. The one-bedroom apartment sat directly above my flower shop and was a little cramped for my taste. I wasn't a hoarder—despite what my mother might say—but I'd collected an array of trinkets and art pieces from my world travels and wished I had enough space to properly showcase them all. As it was, I had three storage boxes wedged into my closet and another one downstairs in the broom closet of the flower shop. Someday I'd have a home of my own and could finally unpack everything into artful displays, rather than shove everything together on the squatty bookcase in my living room.

Using the light from my smart watch, I peeked over the back of the couch. Hayward wasn't there. *Hmm.* That was odd. With a shrug, I went to the front door, not minding my footfalls. My fingertips just grazed the knob when Flapjack's purr cut through the darkness. "Where are you going?"

I stilled, mentally muttering a curse. I wanted to be alone with my thoughts. Something Flapjack would not understand.

I hit the switch beside the door and turned to find the Himalayan perched on the dining room table. I frowned. "What have I said about getting on the table? It wasn't acceptable when you were alive and you don't get a pass now that you're not. Off!"

With a roll of his silver eyes he made a melodramatic show of getting down. "Happy?" he asked as he sat on the floor, his thick tail swishing back and forth like a metronome.

"Overjoyed," I replied flatly.

"Where are you going? It's the middle of the night."

I sighed. "I'm going to a rave. I've been meaning to try Ecstasy for a while now."

Flapjack scowled, his tail still. "Is this about the thing with that nerdy ghost lady?"

"Her name is Loretta," I said, acid in my tone. I folded my arms. "And how do you even know about that?"

"Gwen and Hayward said you were freaked out. He's staying out with her tonight to give you some space."

"Then why are you here?"

The cat flashed his teeth. "Got bored."

"Do I even want to know what you were up to this evening?"

If Flapjack was bored, that meant he'd run out of obnoxious pranks to pull. He particularly liked bothering Holly and the other residents of the Beechwood Manor at the other end of town. I'd given Holly my blessing to put up whatever wards or security measures she wanted around the stately home's perimeter, but she'd waved off my concern and assured me the supernatural residents could more than handle the cantankerous cat.

"Probably not," Flapjack answered, a gleam in his eyes. "Though, it appears the night's not over yet."

"Who said you were invited?"

"How are you planning on stopping me?"

I threw my hands into the air. "Fine. Come along if you want. It's not anything exciting. I'm just going out for a drive."

"A drive?" he repeated, strutting across the living room.

Ignoring him, I opened the front door, then stepped through the door that led to the exterior staircase. Another narrower staircase led directly to my shop below, but I usually used the exterior that led directly to the side parking lot where my delivery van was parked.

Flapjack was already in the passenger seat when I climbed behind the wheel. I frowned at him and turned over the engine. The van rumbled to life and I backed out of the reserved space. Beechwood Harbor had a few late-night spots, but none of them were open at this hour. McNally's Pub closed at midnight during the week, along with the pizza place. A little further outside town, there was a bar that would be open but I didn't want a drink. Or, more accurately, I didn't want a drink with the type that would be hanging around a rural bar at 2:30 in the morning.

That left the beach. I pointed the van toward my favorite lookout spot and flicked on the radio. Some pop song filtered through the speakers. I vaguely recognized it and hummed along. Anything to drown out the whirling thoughts. Flapjack stayed quiet, his tail moving in time with the beat. We drove past Beechwood Manor, and I noted an upstairs window was still lit up.

I glanced at Flapjack, wondering if he was the reason someone was still awake.

"It wasn't me," he said with a scowl. "I've left them alone since you told them about lemons. They've started cleaning the wood floors with this awful stuff." He gagged.

I smiled and kept driving up the hill. A little way away from the manor, there was an informal lookout area that provided spectacular views of the harbor in the day, especially at sunset. However, even at night, I liked to sit and watch the waves rolling along under the moon. There was something grounding about the ocean.

Flapjack glanced at me when I pulled the lever for the parking brake. The engine was still rumbling, sending heat and music swirling around us. "What now?"

"Now, we sit."

He glided through the air and sat on the dashboard. "You didn't do anything wrong, Scar. I know you're beating yourself up right now, but you shouldn't."

I shrugged, not ready to let myself off the hook yet.

Flapjack stilled. "How many whack-job ghosts have we come across? Dozens! Now you finally have a way to help. To do something about the spirits that stay here too long and go nuts. This library ghost"—he paused, shifting his words at my glare—"I mean, *Loretta*, wasn't going to move on by herself. Right?"

I hesitated, but then finally nodded in agreement. "At least, I don't think she would have."

"Then you were doing the right thing. Putting her out of her misery before she could hurt herself or someone else."

I scoffed. "You make it sound like she was a rabid dog or something."

"Wasn't she? In a way?" Flapjack poised the question with a hefty weight. "You add five or ten years and she'd be the next Rosie. And what if you weren't there to deal with the fallout?"

My lips pressed together. Was he right? He'd been at my side for several nasty fights with ghosts over the years. Ghosts who hung around too long after they were meant to go tended to come unhinged, and depending on the amount of power, the results could be quite devastating. Was I simply heading off the inevitable before it came to pass?

"Maybe this is all a part of your gift. You've been twisted up about it since you talked to that voodoo lady in New Orleans. I know you have."

I smiled gently at the cat. We rarely saw eye to eye,

but there was no arguing that he knew me better than anyone. He was the only constant in my life (mostly a constant pain in the butt). He'd watched me grow up, travel the world, and he'd been there when I'd settled down and planted some roots, fallen in love.

"Scar, this power, whatever it's capable of, would normally scare the bejeebies out of me. But I'm not scared, because I know *you*. Your only intentions are good and fair and you'll do the right thing. You've just got to decide how deep you want to go with it."

I bobbed my head as my eyes navigated back toward the ocean.

On the way back to the flower shop, I drove past the funeral home. Karla, or whomever had been awake on the evening's earlier visit, had gone home, leaving the funeral home's interior dark. Yellow light spilled across its façade from the street lights, and two spotlights illuminated the wooden sign posted in the center of the neatly manicured front yard.

"I'm assuming you know about Sabrina too?" I asked Flapjack as I slowed to a crawl before the historic home.

"She's the murdered ghost?"

I nodded, my foot shifting back to the gas pedal. I

picked up speed, still looking up at the funeral home. "I'm worried about her. She's got a lot of emotions, and as we've seen—"

A figure appeared in the headlights. My heart rocketed out of my chest and I slammed my foot on the brakes. The van pulled to the right and stopped right before I hit the woman. Only then did reality catch up with my mind and I realized that it wasn't a human standing there.

It was a ghost.

Sabrina Hutchins, to be more specific.

And she didn't look happy.

"Now that I've got your attention," she snapped, cutting through the hood of the van as she surged forward, stopping just short of sticking her head through the windshield.

"Sabrina, I'm sorry about what happened back at my shop. It was your first meeting. There's a lot to unpack. I'm sure if you come back next week, we can—"

"No! I don't want to be *here* next week. I want out!"

"I'm sorry, but I can't—"

"They said you could!"

"Who?"

"Your friends. The old-timer English guy and the hippie chick."

I looked at Flapjack. His lip was curled back. "Those morons."

I closed my eyes, wishing I'd stayed in my bed.

"I don't know what you've heard, but this isn't something I can do. I can help you try to figure out what's tethering you here, but I can't snap my fingers and send you somewhere else."

It was technically true, but I winced anyway. I hated lying.

"I was murdered!" Sabrina shrieked. "Everyone says that's why I'm stuck here. Please, they already took my life away from me. I can't stay here reliving it over and over."

The desperation in her eyes plucked at my heart strings, but right along with it, it tugged at the nest of worries over Loretta and the depth of my power.

"I don't even know if I could do it again," I sighed. "For all I know, that whole thing was a fluke."

"So it *is* true?" Sabrina snapped, calling out my earlier lie.

I hung my head.

"Scar, we don't have to stay," Flapjack muttered out of the corner of his mouth. "Step on it, we'll be back home in two minutes."

"Please," Sabrina opined. "You're the only chance I've got."

"I'll make you a deal," I told her, holding up one hand to stop her pleading. "I'll come back tomorrow afternoon. And if you still want to go, I'll see if I can help. But I want you to take tonight and tomorrow morning to really think about it."

Sabrina's eyes lit up and she nodded vigorously. "I will. Thank you!"

"Okay." I lifted a hand and gestured for her to scoot away from the van. Technically speaking, I couldn't hurt her, but driving over someone—ghost or not—just seemed wrong.

Flapjack held his peace until we parked outside the flower shop. "Let me handle Gwen and Hayward," he said in a low, almost menacing voice.

"They didn't mean any harm," I started.

"It doesn't matter. You have to guard yourself, Scarlet. You think you have problems now, with ghosts bugging you and pushing your boundaries. If word spreads about your new power, you're going to have more than just restless spirits to worry about."

With that, he hopped out of the passenger side door, leaving me alone with the echo of his warning.

CHAPTER 6

"Unfortunately, we don't have a lot of leads on the case," Chief Lincoln said, his expression still holding onto his initial surprise over my random visit to his office at the police station. "We've not given up on the case, of course, but right now, we've conducted all the interviews, searched the scene, and processed the clues, and we're working on finding the next step forward."

I nodded, trying to mask my disappointment.

The pending appointment with Sabrina had overwhelmed my efforts to work, so I'd ducked out early and left Lizzie in charge of the shop. On a whim, I'd driven to the police station to see if maybe there was some new tidbit or promise of information that I could use to coax Sabrina into staying and seeing through the resolution of her murder.

So far, that plan was up in flames, and I didn't have a backup.

"Who was it you said you spoke with?" Chief Lincoln asked.

Oops. That was my cue.

I'd convinced him to talk about the case based on the premise that Sabrina's family member asked me to look into it. A paper-thin story, but one the Chief bought—at least, to a point.

Judging by the line between his brows, the façade was crumbling quickly.

"Her mother. She called to thank me for the flowers and asked if I'd heard anything."

As much as I hated lying, I had to admit, it came a lot more naturally than in the past. A fact that bothered me.

"Hmm. Well, I'll give her a call if you think I should. Though, like I said, there isn't much of an update."

"Oh, no. That's okay. I wouldn't bother her. I told her I'd call."

Chief Lincoln studied me. "Uh huh..."

I popped up from the visitor's chair across from his desk and snatched my purse off the floor. "Thanks for your time, Chief. I should get going, though. Lots of deliveries to make, you know."

He waved politely as I turned away to scurry out of his office. My cheeks warmed as I cut through the bullpen. I could feel the officers looking at me, wondering what it was I'd been discussing with the chief. I didn't suppose they'd believe we'd been talking about his pending boutonnière order.

Back in the van, I exhaled and sagged against the steering wheel. Chief Lincoln had said Sabrina's neighbor had been the one to find her and call in her murder. I didn't know where she'd lived, only that it wasn't inside Beechwood Harbor city limits. Chief Lincoln was helping the force in Pine Shoals, a neighboring town that was even smaller than the harbor. I'd never been to the small town and didn't have Sabrina's former address. There weren't any handholds available for me to even attempt to grab onto.

"Are we on a stakeout?"

I nearly hit the ceiling at Flapjack's sudden appearance.

He cackled.

"One of these days, you're going to give me a real bona fide heart attack. Then what will you do?" I growled at him.

He smiled. "I fully intend on haunting you even after you're dead, Scar. I figured you knew that by now."

I rolled my eyes. "Wow. I can't wait."

He wheezed a purr-slash-laugh. "Admit it, you're looking forward to it."

"To what? Being *dead*? Shockingly, no. I'm pretty good with things as-is." I shook my head in disbelief. "Honestly, Flapjack, sometimes I think your head got screwed on backward at ghost headquarters."

BIG GHOSTS DON'T CRY

"Think of all the snooping you can do when you're dead," he continued, undeterred. "It's like one big stake out."

"I'm not snooping. And this is not a stake out." I gestured up at the police station. "I was just in a meeting with Chief Lincoln."

"Trying to get info on the dead chick?"

I sighed and leaned back. "In the past, when we've dealt with murder cases, the soul was able to move on as soon as the murder was solved. It's likely the same with Sabrina. If she can just be patient long enough to get the truth, it would be enough to set her free. Without my help."

"Maybe. But there's no guarantee this thing gets solved."

"That's pessimistic."

He tilted his head. "Not every story gets a happy ending, Scar. You know that."

I started the van, still weighing my options. Suddenly, an idea sparked and I perked. My gaze slid sideways and landed on the fluff ball in the passenger seat. "I can't get info, but if I recall, I know someone who's good at getting info from police stations ..."

Flapjack sighed. "What do you want to know?"

Smiling, I turned off the van's engine. "Sabrina's neighbor is the one who found her. I'd like to know what else they might know about her. See if you can find their name and address. If not, then just Sabrina's address will do."

Flapjack muttered under his breath, something that included the words *bad* and *idea*. But he hopped through the side of the van and started up the sloped parking lot that spread out in front of the station.

As he trotted away, I made the mental note to ask where he'd even learned to read. It was one of those questions that came up so infrequently that I always forgot to get around to asking.

Likely because by the time I needed Flapjack to intervene, things were already off the rails and didn't slow down till the final crash, after which I forgot all about the ghost cat's unnatural ability.

The digital clock on the van's dashboard counted off the minutes. Five. Ten. Fifteen. By eighteen, I was ready to drive off without the ghost cat and let him catch up to me later. The only problem was I had no direction. I could head to Pine Shoals, but if Flapjack got distracted or disinterested in the mission—he was a cat after all—I'd be stuck waiting around there too.

Finally, his infuriating little self slipped through the station's front door. He wove through the incoming postal carrier's legs before brushing up against her and flashing his teeth in a grin as she shivered.

"Honestly," I muttered, shaking my head.

He popped into the passenger seat and I glared at him. "What is the matter with you?"

"What?" he asked, feigning innocence. His large eyes went round.

"The *Puss in Boots* thing doesn't work on me, remember?"

He scoffed. "I was just having a little fun. It's not like I can hurt someone by touching them."

"Thank Hades for that. Or whoever it is that comes up with these rules." I turned on the van. "All right, where are we going?"

"Before I give you the information, I think a little negotiating is in order."

My knuckles went white as I gripped the wheel. "Flapjack!"

"Come on, Scar. Sweeten the deal a little." He grinned.

I squinted at him. "I'll buy two cans of tuna, open them, and leave them on the back porch for two days."

"Hmm." He considered it with a slight tilt of his head. "If you leave it outside, I have to contend with all the street cats."

I rolled my eyes. "You think you'd have compassion on those in need."

"In need? Have you seen the size of that black-and-white? His belly drags on the ground. It's unbecoming of a cat."

I shrugged. "I kind of like him."

Flapjack scowled.

The ultimate threat would be adopting a flesh-and-blood feline to reside in the apartment. Flapjack would come unglued. The landlord would slap me with ridiculous fees if I wanted to have a pet, but sometimes

I thought it might be worth it just to watch Flapjack squirm.

This was one of those times.

"Fine," I countered, my tone sharp. "Tuna, in the house, *one* day. Then it gets put outside and you can enjoy it until the others find it. That's my best offer!"

The Himalayan mulled it over, his tail sweeping through the air.

"Flapjack ... " I ground my teeth.

It was already four thirty in the afternoon. I didn't want to show up at some stranger's door right in the middle of their dinner if I could help it.

"Fine, fine, fine. It's a deal."

"Swell." I reached for my phone and mounted it on the magnetized docking station. "Address?"

He rattled it off and I punched it into my GPS app.

"When will the tuna be available?" he asked once we were moving.

"Tomorrow, all right?"

"Fine."

As a ghost, Flapjack couldn't enjoy the taste of fish, but for whatever reason, smelling it was nearly as satiating. He took daily trips to the docks when the catch of the day was brought in, and he still mourned the closure of the town's small cannery several months before.

Personally, if I couldn't actually enjoy something, I didn't want the smell of it to tempt me. It was like trying to avoid sugar, ya know for health and longevity,

BIG GHOSTS DON'T CRY

and all that jazz. If I was sworn off sweets, the last thing I wanted was to walk by a bakery. It was torture! I couldn't fully imagine myself one day wandering the earth as a literal spirit of wanderlust, but if I ever found myself in the position, maybe I'd take to haunting bakeries.

In my experience, stranger things happened. All the time.

Pine Shoals was a thirty-minute drive outside Beechwood Harbor. I played the radio and cringed at Flapjack's off-key sing-along. When we arrived at the address, I parked across the street. To anyone looking out their window, they'd assume I was there to deliver flowers to one of their neighbors. The Lily Pond van was the perfect decoy vehicle, as far as I was concerned.

"Is that one Sabrina's?" I asked Flapjack, gesturing at the house to the left of the neighbor's. Its flower beds were pristinely kept, but from the looks of things, the grass hadn't been mowed in a couple of weeks. This time of year, it dumped rain by the buckets, so the grass could go from manicured to jungle in less than a month. Sabrina's murder had taken place almost two weeks ago.

Flapjack leaned forward, reading the numbers. "That's it."

The police tape had been taken down. I imagined it wouldn't be too long before a For Sale sign was planted in the dense grass. Her parents lived in Minnesota and her ex-husband and daughter had a house of their own in the next town over.

"What's the neighbor's name?" I asked Flapjack, still studying Sabrina's home.

Had she been back to her home since that night? Had she reset to the scene of the crime the night before, after her meltdown in my flower shop? On the one hand, it was her home. Her sanctuary away from the world. But that sanctuary had been violated. Any comfort she might have once found there would be ripped away now. Any happy memories she'd made there would be drowned out by that horrible night. Wouldn't they?

"Barry Wentsworth."

"Any other info?"

"He's the one who found the body. According to him, our ghoul-pal—"

"Sabrina," I corrected, sliding him an evil eye.

"Fine. *Sabrina* had the flu. He was taking her some soup and a few DVDs to borrow. He knocked and she didn't come to the door. He figured she was asleep, so he went back home. A few hours later, he tried calling. No answer. Says he had a bad feeling about it and went back over, went inside, and found her. Dead."

"The door was unlocked?" I asked.

"He had a key. Apparently, he was in charge of her houseplants and cat whenever she'd go out of town for work."

"Oh. Do the cops know how the killer got inside?"

"I don't know."

"Flapjack! You were in there for a good twenty minutes. What were you doing?"

A glint reflected in his silver eyes.

"You know what, never mind. I don't want to know."

I threw open my door and hopped out of the van.

"What's your cover story here, Scar?" Flapjack asked, appearing at my ankles. "You need a good alter-ego name. Hmm. What about Inspector Rose? Florist by day, crime-fighting gumshoe by night!"

"When should I expect the graphic novel?" I deadpanned.

He wheezed a happy purr, satisfied with himself.

It was a valid question though, one I'd toyed with during the drive over. Unfortunately, I hadn't come up with an answer yet. There wasn't a good, plausible reason for me to be poking around in Sabrina's murder investigation, and I sure as Hades wasn't going to start telling people I'd spoken with her ghost. I'd had mixed results with people's reactions to my powers in the past. Some, like Lucas, were positive, though a little cautious. Others offered me fame and fortune. But the vast majority thought I was a nutcase and a possible danger to myself and others. One psychotic break away from a crime spree orchestrated by the voices in my head.

"Hmm. Maybe Inspector Rose is off the table, but *Journalist Rose* could work." I smiled at Flapjack.

"What's that little paper called? You know, the one I use to kill flies in the shop."

"Ah, the little gem that's known as *The Harbor Hubbub*," Flapjack replied, amusement in his tone.

I snapped my fingers. "Yes! Well, for the day, I'm Scarlet Rose, with the esteemed press."

"Impersonating a journalist? Nice. I always knew one day you'd fully cross over to the dark side."

I frowned down at him. "*Fully*? As in, I have a toe over the line as it is?"

"Oh, you have more than a toe, Scar." He smiled. "But that's what I like about you."

He winked out of sight, materializing on the other side of the street after a car passed by. I sputtered a muttered counterpoint under my breath as I marched across the street. "You're wrong," I told him in summary when I reached the opposite sidewalk.

"You really do make it too easy, Scar. It's starting to take some of the fun out of it. Maybe I'll stick to badgering Hayward."

"Ugh! Why I even let you come with me—"

"I'm the one with the address, remember?"

"Yeah, yeah. Well, you're in danger of losing your tuna privileges."

"You wouldn't!"

"Hey," I said with a grin, "you're the one who said I'm walking on the dark side. Seems like just the kind of thing I'd do."

CHAPTER 7

*B*arry Wentsworth was a middle-aged man with disheveled sandy-blonde hair, close-set eyes, and a long, sharp nose. In a weird way, he reminded me of Roger from Disney's *101 Dalmatians*. But, that could have just been the sweater vest and old-school pipe dangling from his mouth.

"Who're you?" he asked, his voice low and gruff.

"Hmm. A prickly pear. Your favorite, Scar," Flapjack said, looking the man over before slipping past his ankles.

I forced my eyes up to meet Barry's and extended my hand. "My name is Scarlet Rose and I'm a reporter with *The Harbor Hubbub*, a local paper in Beechwood Harbor. Do you have a few minutes to talk with me about the Sabrina Hutchins' case?"

"Tell him he needs to hire a maid!" Flapjack called from somewhere in the house.

I cringed.

"A reporter?" Barry said, giving me a once-over. There was nothing leery about it but I took a small step back all the same. "I've already told the police everything I remember from that horrible night."

"Right, well, I'm writing a piece more about Sabrina. Who she was as a person."

"Hmm." Another apprising glance. "You got a card?"

A card?

"Sure!" I said, automatically patting at the pockets of my jeans. "Oh, shoot, you know, I just gave the last one out. Would you like to speak with my editor?"

I pulled my cell phone out, readying to dial and desperately hoping he wouldn't call my bluff.

Barry considered me a moment longer and then shook his head. "That's fine. I don't imagine this will be a long interview?"

"No, no. Just a few minutes of your time."

He stepped back and opened the door wider. "Come on inside. I just put on a pot of coffee if you want a mug."

Hesitantly, I followed him into the house, closing the front door behind me. Flapjack wasn't kidding about the maid suggestion, though. From the looks of things, he'd give any housekeeper a run for their money if they hoped to do their job *and* keep their sanity. The house wasn't just dingy, but cluttered, and held the odor of several days' worth of dirty dishes and empty take-out boxes. From a quick look, it appeared that Barry existed on a diet of delivery pizza, Chinese food, and frozen waffles drenched in syrup.

Flapjack wandered down the hallway off the living room, leaving me alone with Barry.

"How do you take your coffee?" he asked, heading into the kitchen.

"Um, black is fine."

I didn't plan on drinking it anyway.

While he puttered in the kitchen, I picked through the stacks of boxes lining one wall. Old magazines filled at least two dozen banker boxes. *National Geographic*, *Popular Science*, *TIME*, even *People*.

A baby grand piano was the only untouched surface. In fact, as I neared it, I realized it wasn't only free of the clutter that plagued the rest of the room, but it was spotless. Freshly polished to a shine, not a speck of dust on the keys.

"Do you play?"

I whipped around to face Barry as he came into the room, pipe clenched between his teeth as he carried a mug in each hand. He passed one to me, and I noted the chipped edge. The whole picture was confusing. Barry's home was by no means small and resided in a nice neighborhood. The outside was well-maintained and the car in the driveway looked like it was fairly new. But the inside, save the piano, was an absolute mess, and the mugs we held were battered and faded.

"I don't," I answered, gesturing with my free hand

back toward the piano. "It's lovely, though. It's one thing I always wish I'd learned."

"Hmm. My wife was the musician," he explained, his gaze hitched on the piano for a long moment. "What is it you'd like to know about Sabrina?"

We took our seats opposite one another, me on the loveseat, he in a large recliner that appeared to be his usual spot in the large room, judging by the mounded contents of the ashtray set on the small table beside it.

"It's my understanding that you two were friends, is that right?" I started, lowering the mug of coffee to my knee.

"Something like that," Barry replied. He set the pipe aside and sipped from the coffee. "We'd been neighbors for five years or so. We both bought our homes here when they were first built. They're the same floor plan, just mirrored."

I nodded politely. "What was she like? Did she have any hobbies or belong to any clubs?"

"She was a mom," Barry replied. "Sabrina's life revolved around the girl, Miranda. Soccer practice, prom-dress shopping, field trips, PTA, all that."

"Did she enjoy it?"

He offered a small shrug. "Seemed to."

"I read that she traveled often for work."

He nodded to confirm.

"Did she enjoy that? Traveling?"

Barry took a long, thoughtful sip of coffee. "Not really. She didn't like being away from home."

"Sabrina was a nice woman and a good neighbor. She'll be missed around here. You might interview some of the other neighbors for your piece. Everyone in this development is pretty close. There's a monthly potluck dinner at the community clubhouse."

"That's nice," I said with a genuine smile.

Barry shrugged again.

I leaned forward, holding the mug with both hands as I braced my elbows on my thighs. "Mr. Wentsworth, off the record, do you have any idea who might have wanted to hurt her?"

Barry bristled at the question. "It's fairly obvious, isn't it?"

I blinked.

"Cases like these, it's always the same story. The ex!" Barry put his coffee aside and picked up the pipe. He stuck the stem into the corner of his mouth. "They were in a big custody battle. He got some fancy job offer in California, but their original divorce paperwork says he has to stay close enough for Miranda to see him every other weekend. He wanted to give up his weekend visits and take the whole summer, so the girl would go live with him full time in the summer. Sabrina wasn't having it. They were set to go to court next month." He paused and blew out a ring of thick smoke, then pinned me with a serious stare. "With Sabrina out of the way, he wins."

Flapjack strutted back into the room, his tail alert. His whiskers twitched at the smell of pipe tobacco.

"You getting anything out of Beanpole Baggins here, or can we get going?"

I shot a frown at him. "Do you know her ex? Were they married when they moved into the neighborhood?"

"Not for very long. They separated probably a year or so after moving in. As far as I could tell, things were already pretty far gone by that point. He cheated on her and she kicked him out. It should have been cut and dried, but he fought for custody and that dragged out for a long time. It took a toll on Sabrina. Maybe that's why she tried so hard to be super mom."

A sadness clung to the air following Barry's words and my heart sank. I'd give it my best shot, but the glimmer of hope that I'd be able to talk Sabrina into sticking around had turned to dust.

After thanking Barry for his time, I left his home and returned to my van. He watched from the front window of his living room and I offered a friendly wave. He probably thought it was odd that I was climbing into a flower delivery van when I was supposed to be a journalist, but quickly decided it likely wasn't that odd. After all, writing for a tiny local paper hardly conjured the image of champagne bottles popping and a *Scrooge McDuck* pool of gold coins.

Girl's gotta eat.

"Blech!" Flapjack sputtered, waving his tail around as if he could disperse the air around him. "I was about to gag if we had to stay there for another minute. Who smokes that foul stuff? Good luck getting that stench out of your hair and clothes. You're probably going to have to burn that sweatshirt."

I laughed and pulled away from the curb. "Just be glad you don't have literal fur. I'd have to dunk you in the sink."

Flapjack shuddered. "Where are we going now? Are you going to talk to the other neighbors?"

"It'll be five o'clock by the time we get back to Beechwood Harbor. Sabrina's going to be expecting us. Besides, I don't think there's much more we can glean from talking to the other neighbors. At least, nothing that's going to convince Sabrina to stay."

"So, what's the plan then? You're really going to cross her over, like you did with Loretta?"

I exhaled slowly. "I'll hold to my bargain. If I can't convince her to stay, then I'll do my best to ferry her over to the next realm."

Flapjack settled into the passenger seat, his eyes trained forward. "Maybe you should talk to your witchy friend first."

I shot him a look. "What about all that stuff you said last night? About trusting me with this power?"

"I do, Scar. But still … this feels like a big step. What if there is some kind of repercussion we don't know about yet?"

"Like what?"

"That's the point," he countered. "We don't know."

I shook my head. "I don't think so. Maybe if I was trying to shove spirits through, but with Loretta and now with Sabrina, they're ready to go. And like you said, if this is a way to cross over unhappy ghosts, it will ultimately save us and a lot of other people a bunch of problems in the future. No manifesting. No poltergeisting. Just a peaceful co-existence.

"As for Holly," I continued, "she didn't even know what soul shepherding was. That was all Lilah's information. So, as much as I respect Holly's wisdom, on this one, she's out of her depth, too."

Flapjack didn't press his argument. I turned on the radio and we rode back to Beechwood Harbor in tense silence. As much as I tried to rationalize that the only reason I was worried was because I was doing something new, I couldn't fully shake the anxiety away.

A handful of minutes past five, we pulled up in front of the funeral home. "You coming with?" I asked Flapjack.

"I'm in it now," he said, not sounding thrilled about it.

Not that I could blame him.

I climbed out of the van and shut the door, taking a cautious look up and down the street. It was still light outside and would be for another few hours. Not the ideal place to host this reverse-séance.

"I should have told her to meet me at the shop after hours," I muttered.

Flapjack rounded the front bumper and stood beside me. "Maybe she had a change of heart?"

"Maybe."

I'd expected Sabrina to meet us outside, the same place where we'd met the night before, but there was no sign of her.

"Should we go inside?" I wondered out loud. "I could collect any of the vases left behind from her service."

"Worth a shot. But if she doesn't show up in the next ten minutes, I say we get out of here and make a pit stop at the market on the way. You owe me a can of tuna, remember?"

"How could I forget?" I muttered.

Flapjack followed behind me as I crossed the street. "Now, the real question is, albacore or yellow fin?"

I lifted my eyes to the puffy white clouds above, pleading silently for an extra dose of sanity.

"Scarlet? What a surprise!" Karla greeted from behind the large oak desk that sat off to the side of the home's foyer.

"Hello, Karla. I hope I'm not bothering you," I said, closing the door behind me. A gentle chime sounded.

"Not at all. I'm just catching up on paperwork. What can I do for you?"

Before I could answer, Sabrina appeared, floating in from the wall behind Karla. So, she'd mastered at least one of her new ghost skills. That had to be a positive sign. Right?

"I've been waiting all afternoon," Sabrina whined.

I forced my eyes off her and smiled at Karla. "I was just passing by and thought I'd stop in and see if there was anything left over from the service the other night that I could get out of your way."

"Oh, of course." Karla stood. "The family took the smaller arrangements, but they left the two larger ones in the hurricane vases. I'll help you with them—"

Karla stepped out from behind the desk only to be reeled back in when the phone rang. "Shoot. I have to get this. I'm waiting on a call."

I waved a hand. "No problem. I'll be fine. Thank you, though."

Karla smiled, picked up the phone, and sank back to her seat as she answered the call, "Beechwood Funeral Home. This is Karla speaking, how may I help you?"

Not waiting, I scuttled down the hall into the viewing room. It didn't appear they'd had a service since Sabrina's, but the room was clean and smelled of wood polish. The easel was folded against the wall, my florist's foam likely discarded along with the flowers. Two empty hurricane vases were on the antique table off to one side of the room.

Sabrina shimmered into view as Flapjack popped up on the table between the two vases. "I haven't

BIG GHOSTS DON'T CRY

changed my mind!" she declared, almost proudly. "I want you to send me on, to whatever happens next."

I bobbed my head and then quickly licked my lips. I had one last shot to try and change her mind. "I spoke with your neighbor, Barry today. That's why I was late."

Sabrina's face registered surprise. "Why did you do that?"

"I wanted to find out more about your life. He told me that you traveled a lot for work."

She nodded even as her brows pinched together. "So?"

"So, I thought maybe you'd want to do some more traveling. He said you never got to fully appreciate the places you went because you were there on business, but now that's all gone. You could go travel the world, see everything you never got a chance to. My friend Hayward Kensington III could tell you all the best places to see in England."

"Maybe he could be your tour guide!" Flapjack suggested brightly. "You could take him off our hands—I mean, rely on his expertise for months!"

I shot a pointed look at the cat. He gave a wicked flick of his tail, returning my scowl with a grin.

"I told you, I don't want to do any of that," Sabrina replied tartly. "You know, I'm beginning to think you're all hot air."

Karla's voice floated down the hall. She was still on the phone, but there was no way of telling how long she'd be occupied. And I got the feeling that

Sabrina would balk if I suggested a second meeting place.

I glanced at Flapjack.

It was now or never.

Drawing in a deep breath, I held up both hands. "All right. Close your eyes," I told the woman.

Once Sabrina's eyes were closed, I reached out for her hand, just as I had with Loretta. The impulse wasn't there, but when my hand neared hers, a spark of some foreign energy buzzed. The room faded as my vision blurred around the edges. My heart raced into a panicked frenzy and I snapped out of it right before my legs buckled underneath me.

The room spun, and when I blinked away the fog, I realized I was alone. Sabrina had gone; only a slight shimmer remained before she vanished altogether.

My spine stiffened at the sound of footsteps in the hall. I twisted around just as Karla came to a stop in the doorway, a smile on her face.

"Scarlet, did you need a—" she stopped short, the smile melting like hot wax. "What's going on in here?!" she asked, alarm sending her voice an octave higher than normal.

To anyone else, the scene would appear normal. The lights weren't flickering, chairs weren't artfully arranged in a tower in the center of the room, and there were no spooky sound effects accompanying the transition.

At least, that's what I'd thought. Judging by the look on Karla's face, I'd thought wrong.

Her eyes were huge and round and anchored on the place Sabrina had just stood. There was no doubt that she'd just seen the spirit's crossing.

But how?

"Was that *Sabrina?*" Karla asked. Not waiting for an answer, her eyes flashed and then narrowed into slits that threatened to cut me to the core. "What did you do?"

CHAPTER 8

"*H*ow do you—you *saw* that? You saw *her*?" I sputtered, the words a jumbled mess.

Karla folded her arms over her chest. "She told me about this ridiculous plan. I didn't think you'd actually be stupid enough to go through with it!" Karla huffed, shaking her head like an agitated horse. "Honestly, Scarlet, what were you thinking? Do you even realize what you've done?"

Um. No.

But I wasn't going to tell her that.

"Hold the phone!" I barked. "How do you even know about *any* of this?"

Karla took a deep breath, and I got the impression it was the only thing keeping her from flying across the room and throttling me. Her eyes were still angry as they circled back to mine. "I'm a Summoner."

"A Summoner?"

"Yes," Karla snapped. "I'm in a lower class, meaning I can't bring anything from the Otherworld back to this realm, but I can conjure those on the other side and commune with them. Mostly humans, though I've spoken with a demon or two in my day."

My jaw felt permanently unhinged.

"Demons? That's it, I'm outta here," Flapjack said, jumping down from the table.

"I have to admit, a talking cat is a new one, even for me," Kara said.

Flapjack froze.

"How long has he been with you? Is he your familiar?"

I shook my head, blinking rapidly. "Um—he—no. I'm not a witch."

Flapjack sniffed, staring up at Karla. "I'm not anyone's magic security bouncer and I'm not a familiar."

"He was my childhood pet," I explained. My mind was still spinning at three-hundred miles an hour, but the story of how Flapjack had come to be was a story I'd told dozens of times and could recite without much effort. "And, incidentally, my first ghost. I was eight."

Karla studied me with interest, some of the hostility fading. "So, what are you then? If not a witch, what? You don't look like a shifter."

I wasn't sure what that was supposed to mean, but I didn't think it was a compliment.

"I'm a ghost whisperer," I told her. "At least, that's the title I've chosen for myself."

Flapjack gave me a quick look but didn't question my decision to hold back the truth of my power.

"No," Karla said, shaking her head. "That's not it. Or, at least, that's not *all*. I just watched you send a soul forward into the next realm. That's magic. *Powerful* magic. What are you really?"

"Who died and made you the queen of ghost town?" Flapjack asked, stalking toward Karla. "Scarlet doesn't answer to you or anyone else."

"Flapjack—"

The cat didn't heed my low warning. He stopped right before Karla and whipped his tail through the air. "That ghost *wanted* to leave. She begged Scarlet to help her move on. So, that's what Scarlet did. She helped her. That's what she does. She helps ghosts. You got a problem with that? Or is it more that this is your turf and you don't want someone else in the supernatural spotlight?"

Karla stared at Flapjack for a long moment, locked in some kind of staring contest—which, for the record, is never a winning idea, seeing as how ghosts don't biologically have to blink.

"Enough, you two. Listen, Karla, I'm sorry if this crossed a line, but Flapjack is right. Sabrina asked me to help her cross over, and so I did. It's really as simple as that."

Karla's eyes snapped back up to meet mine. She snorted. "Simple? Oh, no, no. This is anything but *simple*. You really have no idea what you've just done, do you?"

I crossed my arms, my hands balling into fists at my sides. "My friend is a witch. She lives here, in Beechwood Harbor. She's never told me about you. And I'm pretty sure she knows all the supernatural—um—*beings* in town."

"I'm not a *being*," Karla said, clearly taking umbrage with the term. "I am a person. And as for Holly, at least that's who I'm assuming you're talking about, she doesn't know everything. I keep my powers to myself. I don't go broadcasting my talents to every vamp, shifter, and ghost in town. Most of the time, the ghosts here don't even know I can see them. I make it a point to ignore them and not interfere with the natural cycle of things."

I frowned at the not-so-subtle dig.

Karla crossed the room, knelt, and folded back one corner of the long aisle runner that stretched between the wooden folding chairs that were usually set up for services. She popped up a loose floorboard and pulled out a shoebox-sized safe. Without looking at me, she dialed in the passcode, opened the door, and pulled out a small canvas satchel.

Flapjack looked up at me and I shrugged.

Karla replaced the safe and the floorboard and

kicked the carpet back into place. She stood and opened the satchel.

"What are you—"

"Shh!" she hissed.

My fists clenched a little tighter as I looked toward the exit. I'd never heard of a Summoner before, but found it hard to believe that Karla could stop me from leaving. My van was parked right out front. I could make a run for it and be back home in five minutes flat. Granted, in a town the size of Beechwood Harbor, it wasn't likely we'd never run into each other again. Could we go on like this night had never happened? Passing with polite, if not guarded, smiles at the store or post office?

I doubted it.

Karla had begun removing items from the satchel and placing them on the door a foot or so in front of the wooden pulpit. With each new object, she formed a small circle, about the diameter of a hula hoop. The objects were all different: a rose quartz, black tourmaline, a blood-red pillar candle, a bundle of some type of dried herb, and a golden pyramid that looked like a gift-store trinket from a King Tut exhibit, but something told me it was far more than a cheesy paperweight souvenir.

When she finished, she placed the satchel on one of the wooden chairs. The circle was nearly complete, but there was a large space between the pyramid and the first crystal she'd placed. Karla stepped to the empty space, careful not to cross some invisible line linking all the objects together. Her gaze looked far away as she lifted her hands and removed the pendant necklace from around her own neck. From across the room, I couldn't see the shape of the pendant and couldn't even remember her wearing it. Which, was odd in itself, as I always had an eye for jewelry, especially funky, unique pieces.

Karla placed the pendant in its place amongst the other items, and no sooner had it touched the floor than a golden line appeared, shooting from one item to the next like a quick flame blazing up a line of gunpowder. When the final line connected, a strange hum echoed through the room and it felt as though the temperature had dropped a good ten degrees instantaneously.

"Scar …" Flapjack said nervously, coming to stand beside me.

Karla looked up from the circle and the golden light reflected in her normally hazel eyes. "I call forth Sabrina Hutchins, who left this world today to cross over. Show her to me!"

Karla closed her eyes and muttered something else in a language I didn't understand. The words were strange and twisted, not like anything I'd ever heard before in all of my travels. Goosebumps broke out along my arms and the hair on Flapjack's back stood on end.

Suddenly, Karla's eyes snapped open and another low hum filled the room.

The circle of light pulsed and then Sabrina's ghost appeared, just as it had been minutes ago before I'd sent her across.

"You!" she demanded, her eyes locking on mine. "What did you do to me? What is this place?"

Karla looked at me, the gold drained from her eyes. "She can hear you."

Slowly, I lowered my arms and took a tentative step closer toward the circle. "Sabrina? Where are you?"

"I don't know, but this is not what I signed up for! It's worse than being there, stuck on earth. At least there I had people to talk to! This place is … empty. Desolate. There's nothing and no one."

"I don't—I don't understand. How could that be right? That can't be all there is on the other side."

Even as I said it, I realized that I had no proof. No one who had crossed over had ever come back—at least, as far as I knew. Sure, every religion had their theories and sacred beliefs about what happened after death, but no one *knew* or could prove what was waiting for all of us once we left this world behind.

Panic fluttered through me. What had I done?

"Karla, what does this mean?" I asked, barely able to muster a whisper.

"Her spirit wasn't ready to cross and you forced her over," Karla said.

Sabrina turned to her. "You can see me? I've tried talking to you for days now!"

"It's not that I'm unsympathetic," Karla told her, "but I have a business to run, a life to live. Do you have any idea how many spirits I see come through here? If I tried to stop and help all of them, I'd never have time for anything else. Besides that, there is an order to things, as I was explaining to Scarlet before calling you here."

"I told you I was leaving!" Sabrina said. "Why didn't you tell me this is what would happen to me if I did?"

Karla shrugged. "For one, I didn't think Scarlet had that kind of power. Sure, I've heard about your affection for ghosts and know all about your support group. It's admirable, really. But I had no idea you'd moved into taking more forceful measures. And secondly, it's not my job to babysit specters."

"Then why are you doing any of this?" I asked, anger seeping into my tone. "You just want to rub my mistake in my face?"

"I'm educating you," Karla said coolly. "Additionally, you've created a problem that needs to be solved. If Sabrina remains in limbo for too long, there's a good chance a demon will find her and use its magic to cross through into this world."

Karla might as well have socked me in the gut with a bowling ball.

"*What?*"

"Think of it this way—normally the Otherworld

and this world are separated by a piece of glass. It's strong and it would take a lot to break through. Your average, garden-variety demon wouldn't be able to punch through. Limbo, on the other hand, is separated from this world by a piece of plastic wrap. It wouldn't take much to pierce the barrier and slide into this world."

Flapjack jerked his head up to look up at me. Terror filled his wide eyes.

"If a demon gets through, they'll first appear here, where Sabrina was shoved through, and then it becomes my problem. So, I'm telling you all this in hopes that you'll set about making this right before that happens."

"Yes, of course! Just tell me what to do," I replied.

"What happens to me?" Sabrina asked, the desperation in her voice raked across my nerves.

Karla lowered her eyes. "The demon will use your soul as its ticket out of limbo and you'll be gone. Forever."

Sabrina broke into sobs and my heart squeezed.

"I won't let that happen," I told her. "How long do we have?"

Karla shrugged. "We could have weeks. It could be months. It just depends on how long it takes a demon to find Sabrina and realize she could be their ticket out."

"What about Loretta?" Flapjack asked, speaking for

the first time since Karla began the circle. "Will she be some kind of demon trap, too?"

"Who is Loretta?" Karla asked, tenseness straining her voice.

I pinched my eyes closed, willing myself to wake up from the nightmare unfolding before me.

"Scarlet?" Karla snapped.

I forced myself to meet her eyes. "Yesterday, last night, I helped another ghost cross over. I think she was ready, but I did—I did the same thing as with Sabrina."

Karla swore, her nostrils flaring. "Any others I should know about?"

I shook my head. "No. Just the two."

"What is her full name?"

"Loretta Mays

"And she crossed over yesterday?"

I nodded.

Karla muttered another incantation in the strange, gnarled language and squeezed her eyes closed. She waited a moment and then repeated the words. Still nothing.

Her shoulders relaxed as her eyes fluttered open. "She's not in limbo. She's moved on properly."

The revelation should have made me feel better—and to a point, it did—but it came with a stab of regret. I should have trusted my gut instincts. With Loretta the whole thing had seemed so natural. *Right*. With

Sabrina, there'd been more force and a nagging voice had chattered at me right up until the final seconds.

Why hadn't I listened?

"How do I help Sabrina?" I asked, stuffing down the self-lecture for another time. "What do I need to do to move her out of limbo?"

"It's simple enough, I suppose," Karla began, considering the spirit trapped in the summoning circle. "You've helped spirits cross over before. This will be no different. It just can't be forced. Sabrina's spirit was held back for a reason. There was unfinished business, something tethering her soul to this place."

"I don't know why," Sabrina pleaded. "Please, you have to believe me."

"She was murdered," I offered. "In the past, I've found that once the case is solved, the spirit is released."

"Do you know who killed you?" Karla asked Sabrina.

The woman shook her head, fresh tears streaming down her semi-translucent cheeks like shining beads of mercury. "I don't want to think about it!"

"You have to, Sabrina," I said gently, approaching the circle. "Please, anything you can remember could be helpful. Unless you think there's something else that was holding you back. Your daughter?"

"I miss her so much," Sabrina whispered.

Tears pricked at my own eyes. "I'm sure you do."

"She'll be okay. She's strong and she has Jeffery. For all his faults, he's a good father."

A memory sparked. My conversation with Barry. "Sabrina, is it possible—"

The circle flickered and another hum, this one lower than the last, resounded in the room.

Karla swore again. "The spell is dying."

"Sabrina, is it possible Jeffery is the one who ... attacked you?"

The ghost's eyes went wide but her form flickered and her words came out garbled. All I could make out was, "... never ... "

Then, she was gone.

The light forming the circle sputtered and faded.

Karla sighed. "Like I told you, I'm a lower class of Summoner. I don't have the magical reserve to hold the summoning spell for long," she said, bending to retrieve the objects from the floor. She grabbed the necklace first and quickly slipped it back over her head. The pendant slipped under her shirt and she collected the other items, placing them back in the satchel.

I exhaled slowly. "When can you call her back here again?"

"It will take a few days before my magic builds up again. I don't practice often and when I do, it takes a toll." She slipped the last crystal into the bag, cinched it closed, and crossed to the corner of the carpet that concealed the loose floorboard. "Come back Sunday night. That should give you time to find out more about her murder. If you're right, and that's what she needs before she crosses over completely, we can give her the details and send her through and close this portal for good."

"And if I can't?"

Karla's eyes flashed. "Then you'd better study up on how to use whatever power you have to send a demon back over, because it will likely kill me before I get the chance to try."

CHAPTER 9

I'd like to think what I did next is the same as any normal human would do upon finding out they'd trapped an innocent soul in limbo-land and was on the verge of ushering a demon into the world.

I went home, had a good old-fashioned freak-out, and then called my boyfriend.

"I'm kind of wishing it was April 1st, so I could chalk this up as a really twisted April Fool's prank," Lucas said when I finished breathlessly recounting the horrible evening to him.

I snorted through my lingering tears. "Me too."

"Whew," he exhaled. "I'm not sure where to start unpacking everything, to be honest."

"That makes two of us." I sniffed and wiped at my eyes.

I was lying on my bed staring up at the ceiling, the

scene playing out all over again in the shadows. "And what if it's not enough? Let's say we can get to the bottom of this thing in time, and then we call her back, tell her what we found out, and then ... nothing happens. Then what? I've known ghosts who took *decades* to move on."

"Any chance the demon coming through would be the *Warner Bros* variety, with cute little horns and a tiny red pitchfork?"

"Considering it has to *eat a soul* to get through to this world, I'm gonna venture a guess and say no."

"Right." A can of soda or beer cracked open in the background, and Lucas took a drink.

Alcohol. Yes. Excellent idea.

"I didn't even know demons were real," I scoffed. "Ghosts? Sure. Witches and werewolves and vampires ... yeah, apparently that's all real too. And now, this."

"Wait, *what?!*" Lucas said, clearly spitting some variety of liquid out along with the question.

I jerked upright and slapped a hand over my mouth.

No. No, no, nooooo.

Cringing, I lowered my hand. "Any chance you can pretend I didn't say that part?"

"Not a chance! Start talking."

"Yes, is there anything I'm *not* going to screw up today?"

Flapjack lifted his head from the pillow beside mine. "Well, considering the circumstances, I wasn't going to say anything, but you forgot my can of tuna."

I rolled my eyes and pushed myself out of the bed. "Yeah, yeah."

"Scar?" Lucas said. "Witches? Vampires? *Werewolves?*"

I supposed it was inevitable that this day would come. It just would have been nice if it could have waited until another time. You know, like when there wasn't the overhanging threat of a blood-thirsty demon invasion.

"I was going to tell you," I started.

"Uh huh."

I slipped from the bedroom and crossed through the small living area to pull a beer from the fridge. Something dark and moody, I decided, running my fingertip along the bottles.

"I've only known for a little while," I continued, grabbing a bottle. I cracked it open using the opener magnet I kept on the fridge and went to the couch. I folded my legs underneath me and tried to decide how to compact everything I'd learned into a bite-sized lesson.

"There are a couple of witches here in town. One that I've become good friends with. Um, Holly. I've probably mentioned her a time or two."

"Holly is a *witch?*" Lucas said.

I could picture him pacing his apartment, one hand raking through his hair.

"Yeah. Like bibbity-boppity-boo."

Lucas swore.

"And she had a vampire roommate and her boyfriend is a dog-shifter—"

"Dog-shifter?"

"You know, this will go a lot faster if you stop repeating everything I say," I mumbled.

"I'm just trying to figure out how this is the first time I'm hearing about any of this. I mean, Scarlet, this is—this is crazy! Please, tell me you're kidding."

I set the bottle of beer aside on the small end table beside me. "I really wish I was."

It wasn't the first time I'd wished I could give my powers away or banish the whole thing to the back of my mind the way Karla clearly had. What would it be like to have a normal life? No ghosts, no magic. Certainly no demons.

As if it wasn't bad enough that *I* had to war with the constant spookiness, now I'd dragged Lucas, a completely innocent bystander, into it. When we'd met, he was ghost-curious and so far, over the course of our relationship, he'd been as understanding and even eager to learn more about my world.

But this? This was one too many stops down the line on the crazy train express.

"Lucas, please, can we just forget I even brought it up?"

"Oh, sure. No problem, Scar. Let me just force wipe it from my mind." He paused for effect. "*Whoop*, there, all done. Now, how about them Yankees?"

I frowned. "All right, point made."

"What did they say about all this? Surely, a witch would have some idea of what to do about a rogue demon."

"I haven't talked to Holly yet. You were my first call."

He scoffed. "Considering my limited powers and my *mere-mortal* status, maybe I shouldn't have been."

"Lucas—"

"I'm sorry. I'm just ... well, I don't know what I am right now. Processing, I guess."

I picked at the frayed edge of the afghan hanging over the back of the couch. "Are you still coming into town Friday?"

Silence.

My heart sank.

I'd known one day all the insanity of my life would drive him away. After finding out about my soul magic, I'd just been waiting for the other shoe to drop. Sure, he said he'd stick around and that I couldn't scare him off, but everyone had their limit to what they were willing to put up with.

Seeing ghosts and constantly having a third, fourth, and fifth wheel to our every waking moment was enough to make anyone run for their life.

Lucas deserved better. If I weren't so selfish, I'd have cut him loose myself.

No. Selfish wasn't the right word.

Terrified.

Not of being alone. Hell, I'd spent most of my life alone.

No, I was scared of just how much it would hurt to say goodbye to him.

"I understand if you don't want to—"

"Scar, don't." His voice was firm but not harsh. "You can't keep setting me up like that. I told you I'm not going anywhere, and that hasn't changed. I was actually checking my schedule. I have a meeting tomorrow morning but nothing formally planned for the afternoon. I'll head out after lunch and be there by dinner. Okay?"

A lump formed in my throat and I nodded, unable to speak.

"That is, if you'll have me an extra day," he added, a lightness returning to his tone.

"Of course," I replied. "I'll see you then. Come to the shop first. I need to catch up on work since I played hooky today."

"You got it. I'll see you then. Try and get some sleep."

"I will."

"I love you, Scarlet."

My chest squeezed. "I love you, too."

As it turned out, sleep wasn't in the cards. After trying herbal tea, a white-noise soundtrack on my phone, and a spritz of lavender-scented perfume across my pillowcases, I gave up the fight, dressed in leggings and a faded old t-shirt, and went downstairs to my studio.

The whiteboard showed a handful of orders that were waiting to be completed. We were still in the lull before wedding season, and it was fairly easy to keep on top of things, but I needed to work, to do something, before I had another breakdown. I marched to the walk-in cooler and started pulling five-gallon buckets of flowers. Carnations, lilies, daisies, roses, and bundles of hydrangea.

Flapjack stood on my work table when I lugged out the final bucket. "Little late, isn't it?"

I tucked a strand of hair out of my face. "Couldn't sleep. Figured I might as well get some work done."

He sat down slowly and wrapped his full tail around his front paws. "You gotta give yourself a break, Scar. You didn't know."

Nodding, I turned to get a vase for the first arrangement. "I know."

"So, you're not down here beating yourself up?"

I frowned. Flapjack's constant companionship had its drawbacks, chief among them being that he knew me all too well and could pin me down with barely any effort. Though, the constant seafood demands and sarcastic commentary could wear thin too.

My gaze drifted past him, stopping on the giant overgrown houseplant in the corner. It had started off as a tiny mystery plant I rescued from the market's clearance rack. Though, looking at it now, you'd think I'd fed it a handful of magic beans.

Which, I guess in a way, I had.

Only, *I* was the source of the magic.

I still wasn't sure how it all worked. Holly had given me a book of spells and when I'd been practicing, the plant picked up the magic and went berserk. The darn thing wouldn't stop growing and I'd had to move it out of my kitchen before its vines reached the floor.

During my time in New Orleans, I'd met a young woman who'd revealed that I was more than a ghost whisperer and was the one who'd introduced me to the term *Soul Shepherd*. According to her, my magic held power over the force of life. I could channel the energy of a soul. It was a rare gift and not one I'd ever wished for with a lucky penny, but here it was anyway.

And now, I'd seen firsthand just what it could do.

"Lucas is coming into town tomorrow," I told Flapjack, blinking back into focus. I took the vase to the sink and turned on the tap, waiting for the water to warm a little. "He'll be here through Monday. So you and Hayward need to be on your best behavior. I don't want to spend the entire weekend breaking up your bickering matches."

Flapjack cocked his head. "I don't know why you're

telling me this. Seems old stuffed-shirt might be the one you want to talk to. He's the one who starts it."

I scoffed, unable to hold a smile as I shook my head. I filled the vase halfway and took it back to the table. "Where are they, anyway?" I asked, reaching for a handful of boxwood. "I guess we should fill them in on the situation. Lucas will be here and he's going to help. But it's an *all hands on deck* situation, I'd say."

"They're at McNally's," Flapjack said. "Karaoke night."

I stilled, one sprig of boxwood poised over the vase. "*Hayward* is singing karaoke?"

Flapjack snorted. "Would I be sitting here talking to you if he was?"

"Good point."

Once a month, the pub stayed open till 2 a.m. for a town-wide karaoke contest. I'd gone once or twice, and let's just say that no one in Beechwood Harbor was going to be featured on *The Voice* anytime soon.

"Gwen's in a singing group now," Flapjack continued. "The Spice Ghouls."

"You're kidding?" I laughed. "Which one is Gwen? Sporty? Baby? Hmm … she's really more of a Ginger, isn't she?"

"They're all Scary, if you ask me. Believe me, you're not missing anything. It's ear-bleedy."

"*Ear-bleedy?*" I raised an eyebrow. "Is that a technical term, conductor?"

"Do you like cringe-worthy better? Or, maybe, I

should say their performance has a certain flee-and-run-in-front-of-a-train quality to it?"

I laughed. "It can't be *that* bad."

Flapjack's whiskers twitched.

"All I'm saying is that you need to prepare yourself. Because if The Spice Ghouls win this first round of the competition, you're going to get an invite to sit front-row for the finals." He gave an irritated flick of his tail and muttered, "at least you have ear canals. You can buy earplugs."

"I'll keep that in mind," I said, still grinning. I placed a few more sprigs of boxwood and then went to work cutting down a few long-stem roses to the appropriate length for the vase, working from the tallest point down to create a full, round bouquet.

"We have to tell them eventually," I said after weaving a few more roses into the arrangement. "About tonight."

"I know," Flapjack replied, suddenly serious.

"Are you sure there wasn't anything useful in the police station? Do you think you could go back again and take a second look? I'm not sure how much more I'll be able to get out of Chief Lincoln without raising suspicion. From the outside, I have no connection to the case, or even to Sabrina, besides being the one who did her funeral flowers."

"I'll try. Maybe Sturgeon will go with me. He can move papers around, see if there's something buried in one of the stacks."

Sturgeon was one of Gwen's ghost friends, a former Army sergeant who'd somehow developed the ability to move physical objects in his spirit form. His powers had come in handy a time or two, and snooping around the police station would be the perfect time to ask the grizzled veteran for a favor.

"I'll take Lucas and go back to Sabrina's neighborhood. We might be able to get a broader picture of her life if we chat with a few of the other neighbors. If they're as tight knit as Barry made it sound, someone might have a lead."

Flapjack nodded, but there was a worried droop in his whiskers.

"We'll figure it out," I said, forcing a glimmer of brightness into my tone as I snipped a few inches off a rose stem and sliced off a stray thorn. "We've had tougher cases before."

Flapjack lifted his brows. "Maybe so, but last time we didn't have a demon chasing at our heels."

I frowned at him and plunked the rose into the vase. "Gee, and here I'd almost forgotten."

CHAPTER 10

"Of course, we had to do an encore. I mean the crowd *demanded* it," Gwen said, grinning from ear to ear as she recounted the glories of her karaoke set the night before. "So, we all got back on stage and we did *Spice Up Your Life*. It was a big crowd pleaser! Even some of the Lucky Lady gals were singing along!"

I shot Hayward a glance. "Really?"

He nodded, beaming with pride at Gwen. "The song was new to me, but quite an ear worm! I've been bopping along to it all morning. Quite bouncy!"

Flapjack snickered. "You should see when he tries to shake his hips. He looks like a geriatric wildebeest."

"I'm not sure I can even picture that," I replied, blinking to clear the images my mind attempted to piece together from the feline's colorful analogy.

Hayward, too busy fawning over Gwen, didn't

notice the cat's insult. Which was for the best. We were on a tight timeline as it was, and their bickering wasn't going to help anything.

Lizzie had asked for the day off, so I was able to speak freely with the ghosts as I prepared the shop to open for the day. I'd done an hour and a half the night before and finally fell asleep a little after two-thirty in the morning. I'd cursed my alarm when it had rung four hours later, but had managed to peel myself from under the covers when the smell of fresh brewed coffee floated down the hall.

Lucas had insisted on buying me a fancy coffee maker when I'd visited him in the city. He claimed it was for his own benefit during his weekend stays at my apartment, which would become more frequent now that he was living three hours away. The machine could do all kinds of tricks, but for the most part, I had it set to brew my vanilla coffee every morning and so far, it seemed to do the trick in getting me out of bed in three rounds or less with the snooze button.

"All right, enough chit chat," Flapjack declared. "Scar has something she needs to tell you guys."

Hayward and Gwen both looked to me, their smiles fading. "What's wrong, Scarlet?" Gwen asked.

"If that Lucas scoundrel broke your heart, I'll run him through with a—" Hayward paused, his thick mustache twitching in agitation as he appeared to search for the right weapon.

"A scabbard?" Gwen offered helpfully.

Flapjack cackled. "A wet noodle, is more like it!"

Hayward glared at Flapjack, his cheeks puffing out under his spectacles. "It would be some kind of sword!" he promised, still scowling at the cat. Turning to Gwen, he softened. "A scabbard is the holder of the sword, Lady Gwen."

"Well either way, I'm sure you'd be very intimidating," Gwen said in all seriousness.

Flapjack opened his mouth but I cut him off, drawing my hand quickly along my neck.

"Oh, fine," he grumbled.

"This isn't about Lucas," I told Hayward. "And he isn't a scoundrel."

Flapjack rallied, his tail swishing. "He resents him because Gwen thinks he's hot."

I slapped a hand over my face, dragging it down slowly. What possessed me to think I could handle all three of them before 10 a.m.?

"Flapjack, focus! Demons, remember?" I snapped.

Gwen and Hayward went still.

"Lady Scarlet? Did I hear you correctly?"

"Yes."

I drew in a deep breath and laid out the events of the night before, shrinking the debacle into as quick of a story as I could manage without leaving anything important out. Hayward and Gwen's horror intensified as they listened, hanging on every word until I finished.

Hayward's mustache twitched again as his eyes

flicked back and forth like an out-of-control typewriter.

"Poor Sabrina!" Gwen wailed. "She's really stuck with no one to talk to?"

"You'd die all over again," Flapjack muttered under his breath.

I glowered at him and he buttoned up again.

"We're going to set this right, but I'm going to need your help."

"You have us assembled!" Hayward boomed. "What shall the first task be?"

"Why do I feel like we need theme songs and some kind of garment made entirely from Spandex?" Flapjack wondered.

Gwen shot her hand into the air, wiggling impatiently. "Oooh, can I pick out the costumes?"

"Yep, it's official," Flapjack quipped. "We're doomed."

I shot him a pointed look before turning a more patient expression toward Gwen. "Let's put a pin in the costume idea for now," I said. "What I really need is some help getting leads. Do you think you and Hayward could go to Pine Shoals and see if there are any local ghosts? And if so, find out if any of them know anything about Sabrina and what might have happened to her?"

Hayward raised his gloved hand in a salute. "Oh course, Lady Scarlet!"

Gwen nodded eagerly. "Consider it done!"

"Great. Thanks, you guys." I paused and glanced up at the clock. "I've got to hold down things here at the store, and then Lucas is coming in sometime this afternoon. Think we can all have dinner together?"

Flapjack tilted his head. "Will there be anything for us? Say, a can of long-awaited tuna?"

I sighed. "Yes. Though, to be clear, I think *long-awaited* is a bit of a stretch. It's been less than twenty-four hours."

"Time moves differently for ghosts, Scar."

"Uh huh." I grinned, shaking my head. I missed the days when I could send him on his way with a prodding of my toes. "I'll sweeten the pot and give you two if you come home with info from the police station."

That got him going. He perked, jumped down from the work table, and scurried through the nearest wall with almost a trot in his fluffy-footed steps.

"We'll be on our way, as well," Hayward announced before valiantly offering Gwen his crooked arm.

Gwen slid her hand through the loop and they exchanged a sweet smile. "You can count on us, Scarlet!"

I thanked them and sent them off. As they vanished through the wall, Gwen's voice echoed back. "This is so exciting!"

I sighed, wishing I had an ounce of her enthusiasm. All I was left with was a twisted knot of guilt and dread. Though, it did help knowing I had the three ghosts helping me.

There was half an hour until opening and everything was in order for the day. Now, all I could do was wait and do my best not to freak out.

By three-thirty, I was walking my fourth customer of the day to the door and contemplating closing down for the day. In another few weeks, the shop would be packed full of tourists and out-of-towners, and I'd be longing for the quiet afternoons where sneaking out early was even an option.

I waved to Mr. Welsch as he scurried away, one hand wrapped around a ticket-out-of-the-doghouse-with-Mrs.-Welsch bouquet straight from the cooler. So far, the ghosts hadn't circled back to provide an update. Technically, we'd made plans to wait until dinner, but with the ghosts, things rarely went according to plan, and I'd expected to hear from at least one of them by now.

I tried not to read too much into their absence and went back to the register. With the punch of a few keys, the drawer popped open and I started counting the till. The bell on the door rang and I glanced up, my usual greeting catching on the tip of tongue as Lucas strode through the door.

Grinning, I popped my hip and braced my fist

against it. "Good afternoon, sir. How's the day treating you?"

Lucas returned my smile as he sauntered closer. He slipped his hands into the pockets of his jeans and shrugged. "Can't complain. Had a bit of a drive, but the view was worth it," he replied, giving me a meaningful look.

Little butterflies swirled through my stomach. "Tell me, are you looking for something specific today?"

His smile widened. "I've kind of got a thing for tall redheads."

I laughed, slipping out of my impromptu character. "Guess you're in luck."

"I'd say." He leaned across the counter and kissed me firmly. "I missed you," he said, one hand still on the side of my face.

Any lingering apprehension about our conversation the night before faded to the background and I kissed him. "I missed you, too."

"How's business? It seems a little quiet around town."

I nodded and went back to counting the till. "After this weekend, things will pick up. Did you notice all the hanging baskets?"

"I did. Nice work."

I smiled. "Thanks!"

He glanced around the shop. "Are we ... alone?"

"For now," I replied. "We're having dinner with the posse."

"Aha."

I filled him in on the plan as I went through the closing procedures. I scanned both sides of the street before flipping the Open sign around to Closed and pulled the chain on the neon sign in the window. Before I locked up, Lucas went back out to his SUV to grab the large duffel bag he usually traveled with. Sure, he could afford a proper suitcase, but he was ex-military and some habits died hard. He was insistent that the duffel could outperform any luggage on the market.

We'd agreed to disagree on the subject.

I locked the shop up for the night, turned off the lights, and led the way upstairs to my apartment. Lucas stashed his bag in the bedroom and then came back out to the living room, where I was firing up a second pot of gourmet coffee.

"You read my mind," he said, gesturing at the chrome machine. "How are you liking it? Is your mind blown? Life forever changed?" he teased, a playful spark in his green eyes.

I laughed. "I don't know if I'd go that far, but yes, it does make things easier in the morning. Thank you."

He smiled. I'd never had someone dote on me with gifts and flowers before, always having preferred to buy things for myself, but with Lucas, it was clearly the best way he knew how to show me how much he cared, so I let him spoil me. Coming from a wealthy family, I'd grown up without needing or wanting anything. Even as an adult, I'd lived an insulted life. I'd insisted on working my way from place to place while I'd traveled abroad, but I always knew there was a safety net in case things unraveled.

Even Lily Pond was a dream financed in large part thanks to my family. My grandmother left me a sum of money when she passed on, and I'd used it all to lease the retail space and attached apartment. I'd run out of inheritance money some time ago, but without it, the flower shop would have stayed a dream in my head rather than the brick-and-mortar walls around me.

When it came to Lucas, I wanted everything to be on even footing. We equally split bills and treated each other, but when it boiled down to it, he had more money than I did. At least, without my parents' backing. He'd spent years running his own security firm and had been contracted by a television network to oversee the security needs of a popular home renovation reality show *Mints on the Pillows*. Things soured, and he'd severed ties with the network after his time in New Orleans and dissolved his company after getting offered a job with the firm in Seattle. It wasn't TV money, but he was still making a good salary, and they'd even paid all his relocation expenses and offered a large signing bonus. I wasn't sure of the exact dollar amounts, but it was enough that he'd bought a new SUV, a few new suits for client meetings, and we'd enjoyed a *very* fancy dinner at one of Seattle's finest restaurants not too long after he signed his contract.

"I have to say, driving into town today, I was scanning every face, waiting for someone to sprout fangs or wings." He shook his head. "I still haven't quite wrapped my head around everything. I keep thinking about the implications it has for my line of work. I mean, how many strange occurrences and unexplainable things could be traced back to ... magic?"

"They do a pretty good job of policing their own," I told him, moving to the cupboard to pull down two mugs. "They have their own CIA and police and government. It's all very organized."

Somehow, I didn't think that helped relieve Lucas's questions. Judging by the look on his face, it only added to them.

I laughed softly and handed him the first cup of coffee. "You look like you need this one more than I do."

He took it, still dumbfounded. "Thanks."

I poured the second cup and replaced the carafe in the machine. "Let's sit. The ghosts will be here any minute."

"I wish I could hear them for myself," Lucas said as we settled onto the couch. He draped his free arm over my shoulder and I snuggled into his side. For a tiny moment, everything was right with the world. There was no threat of demon invasion, lost ghosts, or magic.

Naturally, the moment lasted all of three seconds.

Before I could get too comfortable, the trio arrived, seemingly in a synchronized entrance, floating through the door in a single-file line.

"Oh, goody, boyfriend's here," Flapjack quipped, stalking into the room. "Or, should I call him your scoundrel?"

I narrowed my eyes.

Lucas tensed, sitting a little straighter. "They here?"

"Yes," I replied, leaning forward to place my coffee mug on the table. "All right. Let's get this thing started."

"You want to start with the good news or the bad news?" Flapjack asked.

I looked at Lucas and sighed. "Bad news."

CHAPTER 11

"The bad news is that the leads are going cold and Chief Lincoln's the only one really trying to chase this thing down," Flapjack said.

I frowned. "That doesn't make any sense. It's not even the BHPD's case."

"The reason we took so long is because we all went to the Pine Shoals station to compare notes. They've moved on to chasing down a vandal who's sprayed half the town with these really tacky spray paint murals in the middle of the night," Flapjack continued.

"And *that's* more important than a woman strangled to death in her own home?" I asked, my eyebrows peaked.

"That's why Chief Lincoln is so cranky," Flapjack said. "He came into the Pine Shoals station while we were there and tore their lead deputy a new one. Told him if he was too lazy to track down a killer, he didn't deserve his badge."

I blinked. "Chief Lincoln said that?"

Flapjack smiled. "It was awesome!"

It was hard to picture Chief Lincoln coming unglued. He was young for a police chief, but he was mature beyond his years and didn't have a temper as far as I knew.

"How did it end?" I asked.

"He stormed out and said he'd do the canvassing himself," Flapjack said. "So, we followed along."

It explained why the trio hadn't circled back to the flower shop.

"They followed Chief Lincoln while he interviewed neighbors," I quickly explained to Lucas.

"And that's bad news?" he asked.

Frowning, I shifted my gaze back to Flapjack. "Good point. You said this is the bad news?"

"The bad news is we followed him around while he talked to a dozen people and came up with nothing," Flapjack clarified.

"Oh." I deflated. "He didn't find anything."

"Got it." Lucas sipped his beer. "So, the neighbor you talked to thinks it was the ex-husband? What about him? What's he say about it?"

"Russ Hutchins," Flapjack said. "Guess Sabrina kept his last name. Anyway, he has an alibi and his daughter, Miranda, backs it up. She was staying with him for the weekend and kept the movie ticket stub from their night out. They were in the theater at the time of the attack."

I relayed the info to Lucas. The line between his brows deepened.

"Could he have hired it out?" he asked.

"It's possible," I answered, "but I'm not sure how they'd find out if they don't have enough to get a warrant or bring him in for a formal interview at the station. And if the Pine Shoals PD is distracted by this spray-paint vandal, they might not be digging too deeply."

I exhaled and leaned back in my chair. "Gwen, Hayward, what about you? Did you get anything from the local ghosts?"

"Oddly, the place is a ghost-ghost town. We couldn't find any!" Gwen said.

"No ghosts?" I repeated. "In the whole town?"

I mentally added it to a list of potential vacation spots.

"Do they have any bed-and-breakfasts?" Lucas whispered out of the corner of his mouth, apparently on the same wavelength I was.

All three ghosts frowned at him.

I laughed. "You're not scoring any points here, babe."

He shrugged and went back to drinking.

"So, no ghosts, no leads, and the ex-husband is off the hook." I tapped my nails against the table, my mind whirling. "Remind me what the good news was in all that?"

"The good news is that Sturgeon did a little digging for us and found something in ex-hubby's trash," Flapjack said.

"Where is Sturgeon?" I asked, glancing around, halfway expecting him to be lurking in a corner somewhere. He was deadly silent—even for a ghost.

"He had to go. Poker night," Flapjack explained. "But he left it out on the porch. He couldn't bring it in through the wall."

I straightened. "He brought it here?"

"What else were we supposed to do with it?" Flapjack asked. "Leave it there?"

I sighed and pushed up from the table. "Yes! The police can't use it as evidence if it's been tampered with."

"Scar, what are we talking about?" Lucas asked, twisting in his chair as I went to the door.

I opened it, found a small phone on the welcome mat, and frowned. "This."

Lucas was at my side in ten seconds, staring down at the phone. "Looks like a burner phone."

"Let me get some gloves," I said, hurrying to the kitchen. I pulled a pair of hot pink rubber gloves out from under the sink. They went to the elbow and were lined with a soft floral print. I handed them to Lucas and he laughed. "Not really my style, but all right."

I rolled my eyes. "You'll know what to do to download the information."

He took a glove and stuffed his right hand into it, cringing at the tight fit.

Flapjack cackled as Lucas donned the hot pink gloves. "Maybe we could find him an apron and a little hat, too!"

Hayward's mustache twitched as he struggled to contain a laugh.

I shot them both a warning look.

Lucas plucked the phone from the mat with his gloved hand and flipped it open. Miraculously, there was some juice left in the battery and the tiny screen lit up. "No contacts," he said, tapping the silver buttons. "No nothing, really. A few outbound calls, all to the same number. No inbound calls. He might have had the number jammed so it would come up as unlisted. Scarlet, can you get me a pad of paper?"

I went back to the kitchen, tossed the spare glove into the sink, and then dug a small pad and a pen from the catch-all drawer under the microwave.

Lucas jotted down the phone number along with the dates and times of the calls. When he laid the pen down, he did one more scan through the phone, and then snapped it closed. "That's everything."

"Is Sturgeon coming back to collect it?" I asked Flapjack. "After poker?"

"Poker?" Lucas repeated. "I didn't know ghosts

could play poker. Maybe this whole death thing won't be so bad after all."

I rolled my eyes.

"Why would he come back for the phone?" Flapjack asked.

"It needs to go back in the trash, and I'm certainly not driving all the way to Pine Shoals to go reverse dumpster diving in the middle of the night."

Lucas looked to me and wiggled the phone.

"Put it back on the mat," I directed.

Flapjack heaved a long-suffering sigh. "I'll go tell Sturgeon to take it back. He's not going to be happy about it though."

"All right, so to make sure I'm following," Lucas said, coming back to the table after replacing the phone and removing the glove, "the ex-husband has an alibi, the daughter, but he's also got a mysterious burner phone in his trash?"

"Yes," Flapjack and I said at the same time.

"It had to have been charged up recently," Lucas said. "There was over half the battery left, but the last call was made two weeks ago. If he used it to contact some hit man, why would he keep it around all this time?"

"I don't know. Could he have scrubbed other data off it?"

"It's possible. I know a guy who could try to hack it, but he's all the way in Chicago. It would take a couple days to get the phone to him, even if we overnighted it."

"Right." I sighed and looked down at the pad where Lucas had written the number. "Should we call it? See if anyone answers?"

"I have a better way," Lucas said.

Without further explanation, he ducked into the bedroom and came back with his laptop. "I have a program that can do a reverse lookup."

"Oh, right. I forgot, I'm dating a part-time super spy."

Lucas chuckled and opened the computer. "I must have left my cape in my other duffel bag."

"It's for the best," I teased. "It would only slow us down."

Flapjack groaned. "You two are insufferable."

Hayward cleared his throat. "Perhaps I'm being daft," he began. Flapjack opened his mouth but I silenced him with a look before he could pounce on Hayward. "But I'm not sure I understand why this phone is so strange. Isn't it possible he simply got a new one and threw the old one away?"

"It's a burner phone," I explained, "which means it's not attached to some kind of phone carrier and is basically untraceable. That on its own wouldn't necessarily mean anything, but the fact that it's clearly in working order but was thrown in the trash seems a little strange, as though the phone served its purpose and was now worthless."

"Why would the ex-husband want to kill Sabrina?" Gwen asked.

"When Flapjack and I spoke with Sabrina's neighbor, he told us the exes were locked in a pretty nasty legal battle. He wanted to move out of state for an important job offer and Sabrina wasn't allowing him to change their custody agreement. Now, with Sabrina dead, he gets full custody and can do whatever he wants."

"Looks like he'd be saving a bundle, too," Lucas added, his fingers flying over his keyboard. "I just pulled up their divorce settlement. Sabrina was getting eight grand a month from Russ."

"Eight grand?!"

Lucas nodded. "They separated three years ago. But the divorce was only finalized eighteen months ago. It took over a year to hammer out the deal. The eight thousand dollars is a combination of alimony and child support, but even once their daughter turns eighteen, Russ will still fork out over four thousand a month to his ex for another seven years."

I shook my head, trying to add up the total sum. "Wow. She must have had a killer lawyer."

"If that isn't the perfect case for a pre-nup, I don't know what is," Lucas muttered under his breath.

My brows crinkled together as I stared at him. "You'd get a pre-nup?"

He looked up, a startled look on his face. "Sure. Why not?"

I scoffed. "That's kind of depressing, isn't it? You're planning for the marriage to fail before it even starts."

Flapjack flicked his tail, a slow grin spreading on his face as he leaned in. "Oooo, this just got *good*."

I shot him a sideways scowl.

"I—I didn't mean anything by it, Scar, but yeah, I think if you're rich, it's a good idea."

"Well, let's say it was us. You have your TV money. I have my inheritance, most of which is tied up in the business. Would we—" I stopped myself, realizing two things. One, we had an audience. Two, we'd never formally talked about marriage, let alone any of the steps that might get us there.

"Never mind," I said quickly before he could answer. "What's going on with the phone numbers?"

Lucas stared at me for another long moment before dropping his gaze back to the screen. "No hits yet on the numbers. It's still processing."

"All right. Well, in the meantime, let's get some food ordered." I jumped up from the table, my cheeks still warm, and scurried into the kitchen. I pulled open the drawer under the microwave and flipped through the take-out menus from the local eateries. "You want something from McNally's? There's probably a thirty-minute wait. Pizza would be faster."

"Scarlet," Lucas said.

"Hmm?"

When he didn't answer, I looked over at him. He was watching me with a conflicted look on his face. I raised my brows expectantly and he jerked upright. "Can you, uh, watch this? I need to use the restroom."

My heart sank. "Sure."

He got up and took long strides across the living room. "And, pizza sounds good. Our usual."

Seconds later, the bathroom door closed.

I raked my fingers through my hair, wishing I'd kept my mouth shut.

Flapjack sighed. "Sheesh, way to spook the herd, Scar!"

"She didn't *spook* him," Gwen insisted, scowling at the cat. "Lucas isn't going to scare off just because you brought up marriage."

"You sure about that?" I mumbled, casting a glance toward the short hallway he'd just ducked into.

Gwen chewed the corner of her lip.

I drew in a deep breath. "It's fine. I'm going to order some food. We'll see if we get a hit on the phone numbers. Was there anything else?"

Flapjack shook his head.

"All right. Well, thanks, guys. And thank Sturgeon, too." I grabbed my own phone off the kitchen counter and held up the menu for the pizza place down the street. "I think we're going to call it a night on the PI stuff for the night."

"That's our cue," Flapjack said grumpily. "We're getting the boot."

Hayward rose and automatically offered his arm to

Gwen. She slipped her hand through it and then gave me a quick smile. "Have a nice night, Scarlet. Everything is going to be fine."

I attempted a smile in return, but it felt forced. "Thanks, Gwen. You too."

They turned away, heading for the door. Hayward said something to Gwen as they slipped through and one of the hushed words sounded a lot like *scoundrel*.

I sighed and flopped onto the couch.

Lucas reappeared moments later and went to the table to lean over his laptop.

"Anything?" I asked.

"Does the name Scott Putnum mean anything to you?"

I considered it for a moment, then shook my head. "I don't think so. Is that who Russ was calling?"

Lucas nodded, his fingers flying back into action. I waited impatiently as he worked. After a few minutes, his computer spat out a *ping* sound and Lucas swore. "Well, I don't know much, but he's got a record. Aggravated assault. Looks like he only got out of prison six months ago."

Lucas straightened and gave me an earnest look. "And what better place to get a world-class education in being a hit man than inside the slammer?"

A strange mixture of hope and dread churned through me. "Sounds like we got our guy. What next?"

"I think we need to pay a visit to Mr. Hutchins and

see why he was having secret conversations with a violent felon."

Sure. What could go wrong?

CHAPTER 12

*G*wen winked into the kitchen the next morning as I put on a pot of coffee. She'd perched herself on the counter beside the fridge, and I nearly dropped the glass carafe of cream when I closed the door and found her there.

I swore loudly and then winced. Lucas was still sleeping soundly in the other room. "Gwen!" I hissed, adjusting my volume. "How many times do I have to tell you guys not to sneak up on me?!"

She smiled. "Sorry."

Grumbling under my breath, I poured the cream into my first cup of coffee and then replaced the small container in the fridge. "Why are you here so early? Isn't this prime time at the Lucky Lady?"

The Lucky Lady Salon was Gwen's favorite haunt. She floated around, slurping up all the gossip and small-town drama like it was sweet nectar. Personally, I couldn't understand the appeal. Whenever I'd gone in for a trim, it was a bunch of ladies complaining about their husband's fashion sense or inability to see items right in front of their faces when looking for food. Occasionally, there were younger women, though they mostly bemoaned the lack of decent shopping options and eligible men in Beechwood Harbor.

"It's book club today," Gwen said. "They're all at Hannah Wesell's place, drinking mimosas and watching *Magic Mike* for the dozenth time."

I blinked.

Gwen laughed at my puzzled expression. "They just tell their husbands it's a book club so they won't tag along or ask too many questions. Normally, they catch up on *The Bachelor*, but it's the off season, so Channing Tatum has worked back into the regular rotation. Not that I'm complaining. The man is basically a walking sculpture."

I sat down at the kitchen table and started on my coffee. If I was going to keep up with Gwen, I'd need every last drop. "You still haven't answered my question. What are you doing *here*?"

Gwen swooped across the kitchen and effortlessly floated into the chair across from mine. "I wanted to come make sure you were okay."

"Why wouldn't I be?"

She shrugged. "Last night, things with Lucas seemed a little ... tense."

I frowned. "You want to know if we talked about getting married."

Gwen innocently batted her long lashes. "Only if you want to talk about it."

"Well, I don't," I told her. "Actually, I take that back. It's not that I don't want to talk about it, it's that there's nothing to talk about."

"Does it bother you that he wants a pre-nup?" Gwen asked, undeterred. "It's kind of Hollywood, don't you think?"

"If by *Hollywood* you mean high-maintenance and unnecessary, then yes, it's very Hollywood."

Gwen cocked her head, her eyes narrowed. "You're grumpy this morning. Why is that?"

"Gwen, it's eight o'clock, I haven't had my coffee, and you're in here peppering me with questions about marriage. It's just a little too much right now."

"Hmm." She straightened and placed her folded hands on the table.

"What are you doing now?" I asked, eying her cautiously.

"I'm waiting until you've finished your coffee."

"Oh for the love of begonias!" I set my coffee down. "I don't care that Lucas wants a pre-nup. It's probably the smart decision, from a logical standpoint, that he protects himself legally. My parents will probably require me to have one anyway, so really, it's saving me an argument with them, if and when it ever came down to it. But honestly, this whole conversation is ridiculous because Lucas and I are not engaged!"

"Do you want to marry him?"

I sputtered at the simple question. "I—we—I mean, maybe, someday, if things were headed that way, we could—"

"Scarlet," Gwen interrupted, tilting her head again. "Yes or no, first thing that comes to mind. Do you want to marry Lucas?"

I pressed my lips together.

Gwen raised her eyebrows.

"Fine! Yes. I think."

Gwen squealed.

I shushed her before remembering Lucas wouldn't be able to hear her, then was struck with how truly insane my life was and started laughing.

"This is ridiculous," I told her.

She bounced in her seat, rubbing her hands together. "Think of the wedding plans! You've probably got the flowers all picked out in your head, but there's the dress and the church and the cake! I like those cakes where they have the little plastic people on top. Why don't people do those anymore?"

"Gwen! Slow down!" I almost reminded her to take a deep breath, but caught myself in time. "This is all just wild speculation. Lucas hasn't even hinted at marriage. I'm not even sure he ever plans to marry."

That dampened her celebration. She sank back into

her chair, her smile fading. "Well what would you do then?"

I sipped my coffee. "What do you mean?"

"If he doesn't want to get married and you do?"

I exhaled. "I'm not worried about that right now. We haven't been together that long, and he just started a new job, and I've got all this ... magic crap to figure out. It's okay if we wait."

"Would you leave Beechwood Harbor?" Gwen asked, suddenly sober.

The question was simple enough, but it somehow hit me upside the head from left field and I hesitated. "I—I don't know, Gwen. I honestly haven't thought about it."

The bedroom door opened and I snapped my mouth shut. Footsteps sounded and then the bathroom door closed.

"That's Lucas," I whispered.

I don't know why I thought she'd take the hint and clear out. Before I could make my meaning clearer, the door opened and Lucas shuffled into the living room. He wore a pair of flannel pajama bottoms and nothing else. He ruffled his tousled hair and scrubbed his hand down his face before looking at me. "Mm. Good morning, baby. Coffee smells good."

Gwen's jaw nearly unhinged as she stared at him, the look in her eyes similar to the one Flapjack got near the fish section of the grocery store.

I cleared my throat and she snapped out of it. "Hmm? What, Scar? What were you saying?"

Silently, I tossed my head toward the front door.

She frowned but levitated from the chair and soared through the room. "This conversation isn't over," she warned before sliding out the front door.

"How'd ya sleep?" I asked Lucas, propping my feet up on the chair Gwen had vacated.

"I'm not gonna lie, I think the bed at my new place has spoiled me for all other beds," Lucas teased, going to the coffee maker.

I smiled. "We can't all have the full Marriott experience."

He laughed.

"What are the odds I can talk you into making your buttermilk pancakes?" I asked, shifting my attention back to Lucas. "You always get them fluffier than I do."

Lucas grinned and poured a cup of coffee for himself. "That's because I'm patient and wait for the baking powder to activate before I start cooking them. You just throw a big glob in the pan and hope for the best."

I scowled at his back but kept my peace. Mostly because I wanted pancakes.

Lucas chuckled. "I can feel you glaring, by the way."

"I'll make you a deal," I said. "You make the pancakes now, and I'll buy lunch later."

Lucas reached into the cupboard where I kept my mixing bowls and pulled the largest one down.

I grinned and finished my coffee while he went to work on the batter.

"Who were you talking with?" Lucas asked, glancing over his shoulder at me. "I heard you out here chatting."

My cheeks warmed. Just how much of my side of the conversation had he picked up on? Mentally, I replayed as much as I could remember. *Yikes.*

"Um, Gwen. She stopped by for a few minutes. She's gone now. Come to think of it …" I paused and craned my neck to peek over the back of the couch. Empty. "No one's here."

Where were Flapjack and Hayward?

"Were you talking about me?" Lucas asked, casually whisking together the batter.

My heart thumped a little faster. "Ego much?" I teased.

He laughed and pulled a frying pan out of the cupboard, turned on the stove, and dropped a little butter in when it got hot.

While he waited for it to melt, he poured me a second cup of coffee.

"Thank you."

He reached up and tipped an invisible cap. "Gratuities gladly accepted."

I laughed. "I'll just bet. My tip rides on whether or not my syrup is warm."

Lucas chuckled and returned to the stove. "Noted."

He poured a cupful of batter into the pan and it

sizzled, sending the sweet aroma through the kitchen. I reached for my coffee mug and tried to keep my drooling to a minimum.

Snippets of the conversation with Gwen floated back to me as I watched him work. There was no question I loved Lucas, and I certainly wouldn't object to waking up with him every morning. But a wedding? Was that what I wanted? As a florist, I spent a good majority of my time in the wedding world, and sure, sometimes I envied the happy glow of the brides I met with for floral consultations. But that didn't mean I was ready to plan a wedding for myself. Not to mention all the complications after that. Lucas was closer now, but we were still separated by over a hundred miles, and that wasn't likely to change any time soon.

I shook my head, banishing the thoughts for the day. Lucas and I were planning to drive into Pine Shoals to confront Sabrina's ex-husband that evening and needed to prepare. Thoughts of weddings bells and happily ever after would have to wait. Assuming we made it out unscathed.

CHAPTER 13

The burner phone was missing from the welcome mat when we left the apartment that afternoon, and I made a mental note to thank Sturgeon next time I saw him around town. Without his search, we'd be chasing our tails, still looking for a lead to follow up on. Lucas drove us to Pine Shoals in his SUV, and we parked on the opposite side of the street from Russ Hutchins's large hillside estate. His home stood in stark contrast to Sabrina's. I wasn't sure what Russ did for a living but judging by the estate and the massive sum he'd been forking over to his ex-wife, it was clear business was going well.

Lucas gave a low whistle. "Looks like he's not hurting, even after the alimony and child support."

I nodded. "I was just thinking the same thing."

"Do you think he'll be home?" Lucas asked, glancing

at the clock on the dash. It was Friday afternoon, right after two o'clock.

"I called his office to see if we could make an appointment, but his receptionist said he was out for the day. He has to come back eventually." I leaned forward and tugged at the zipper on the backpack sitting near my feet. "Which, is why I brought snacks."

Lucas grinned. "An old-fashioned stake out, huh?"

"Yeah, but we're driving back into town if I need the bathroom," I declared.

"Fair enough." He chuckled. "Let's go knock and see if anyone answers."

We climbed out of the car and went across the quiet street. The home was in a neighborhood, but there was a good deal of distance between the properties. Russ's home featured a long, tree-lined driveway, but it wasn't gated. Small mercies. Lucas took the lead and we started up the sloped driveway. A three-car garage was attached to the house, but it was impossible to tell if there were cars inside.

Lucas rang the doorbell and we waited.

Moments later, the door opened and a middle-aged man with tanned skin, sandy brown hair, and an angular face appeared. "Can I help you?"

"Are you Russell Hutchins?" Lucas asked.

The man glanced at me and then back at Lucas. "I am. Who are you?"

"Lucas Greene. This is my associate." He gestured at me but didn't use my name. "We'd like to ask you a few questions about your ex-wife's murder, if you have some time."

Russ balked. "Are you cops?"

Lucas shook his head. "PI."

His answer caught me off guard, but I masked my surprise.

"Private investigators?" Russ laughed, the sound cold and patronizing. He ran a hand along his jaw, smiling in disbelief. "Unbelievable. They're really not going to let this go, are they?"

When Lucas didn't answer, Russ leaned in, any hint of humor gone. "You tell Gerald and Winnie that I had nothing to do with Sabrina's murder. I don't know anything more than what I've already told the cops. You can ask them—they'll tell you I've fully cooperated. And now, I have nothing left to say."

"I see," Lucas said calmly.

Russ tensed, his smile gone. "You know what? You need to tell them to leave this alone, for their granddaughter's sake. How is Miranda supposed to move past this when it keeps getting dredged up over and over again?"

"We're trying to help solve the case," I interjected. "Don't you think the closure would help Miranda?"

Russ looked at me but quickly dismissed my question. "What she needs is to be left alone. Gerald and Winnie are lucky that I've been understanding with their ridiculous accusations. But if this keeps up, I'm going to have to rethink their role in Miranda's life. You make sure they know that."

The threat was red hot and I swallowed hard.

Lucas didn't back down, his face impassible, like cold steel. "Does the name Scott Putnam mean anything to you?"

Fire blazed in Russ's eyes. "This is private property. You need to leave before I call the real cops."

He didn't wait for us to comply before slamming the door in our face. A decisive *click* followed.

"Well, that went well." I exhaled.

"Who are Gerald and Winnie?"

"Sabrina's parents," I said, turning back to face the street.

Lucas nodded, as though he'd expected that answer. "So, they think Russ is good for it, too?"

"Sure sounds like it."

With a final glance over his shoulder at the looming house, Lucas exhaled. "Looks like we need a new angle to get info. We just burnt that lead."

"Should we try to talk to Scott Putnam? Go straight to the source?"

The idea alone made me nervous. Lucas pulled the full criminal record and it appeared he'd served time for two counts of aggravated assault following a domestic dispute with his ex-girlfriend and her new boyfriend. Both the girlfriend and boyfriend ended up in the hospital, and Mr. Putnam went to prison for three years. If there was an angry bear I didn't want to poke, it was Scott.

Lucas shook his head. "Not yet."

We headed back to the SUV.

"Quick thinking with the PI thing," I told him.

"It wasn't actually a lie," he said. "I got my license a while back. I thought that might be what I wanted to do, back before I got into private security."

"Oh. Good to know."

The conversation with Gwen flashed back into my mind. There was still so much we didn't yet know about each other. How many other surprises were left to uncover? And shouldn't we unearth all of them before deciding on something as permanent as marriage?

We stopped at the end of the driveway to wait for a passing school bus. Air brakes sounded and the bus pulled to a stop in front of the Hutchins' house. When it pulled away, a teenage girl with strawberry blonde hair stood opposite us.

"Is that Miranda?" I whispered.

As the girl neared, the question answered itself. There was no denying the girl was Sabrina's daughter. They had the same eyes and noses.

"Hi," Miranda said shyly as she approached.

"Hello," I replied. "Are you Miranda Hutchins?"

The girl gave a tentative nod. "Yes. Do I know you?"

"I knew your mom," I told her. "I'm so sorry for your loss."

"Oh." The girl's face fell as her gaze drifted to the sidewalk. "Were you dropping off a casserole?"

"Um, no," I replied slowly.

Miranda glanced up. "That's usually why people come by. We have at least six lasagnas in the fridge, and the freezer is full of casseroles."

I smiled sadly. "I see."

Miranda adjusted her backpack straps and considered Lucas. "You a cop or something?"

He shook his head. "No."

"You look like one."

I smiled. "Lucas runs a security company."

"Did my dad order a new system or something?" Miranda asked. "Some kind of feature for the new owners, I guess."

"Is the house for sale?" I asked.

Miranda nodded. "The listing should be up next week. The real estate agent was here a few days ago, taking pictures." The teen frowned. "She made me take all my posters down. She said they were distracting, but I think she just doesn't like movies."

"I used to keep posters in my room, too," I told her. "Where are you moving to?"

"California," Miranda answered. "My dad got a job offer down there a while ago. He just couldn't take it until now."

"That's right. I think Sabrina mentioned it."

Miranda scoffed. "That doesn't surprise me. She told anyone who would listen for more than a few minutes, but if *I* asked about it, she wouldn't answer any questions."

"That must have been frustrating," I replied. "But I'm sure she was just trying to keep you focused on school and didn't want to put you in the middle of anything."

"Oh, I was in the middle anyway." She breathed a hollow laugh, shaking her head in disbelief. "They thought they were keeping me out of it, but I'm not an idiot. I could hear them arguing on the phone all the time. Half the reason I wanted my driver's license was so we didn't have to do the pickups and drop-offs anymore. Once I could drive, they wouldn't have to see each other anymore."

I winced. "It was that bad?"

She nodded glumly. "I know it wasn't my fault they got divorced, but I was the reason they had to keep seeing each other, and every time they did, it was a bad day."

"I'm sorry, Miranda. That's awful."

My own parents weren't the picture of marital bliss, but I couldn't remember them ever having full-on verbal battles. At least, not in front of me.

"Was it always about the custody arrangement?" I asked.

"Most of the time," Miranda replied. "But sometimes they'd drag everything else into it. My dad's affair, my mom's OCD. All that crap."

"So, you wanted him to move?"

She wrapped her arms around herself. "I would have missed him, but it sounded cool having a place by the beach. And it would have stopped the fighting."

My heart hurt for the girl. It couldn't have been easy to be stuck in the middle of her parent's game of tug-of-war.

"Plus, it would have forced my dad to move on. He hasn't even started dating again."

"You want him to start dating?" I asked.

She nodded. "He doesn't do well on his own. He works too much and eats like crap. He's going to give himself a heart attack."

"Was your mom dating again? I don't remember her mentioning anyone special."

"There was one guy. She didn't want me to know," Miranda said, her delicate features crinkling. "I broke my cellphone and she had me use hers while I waited for the company to send me a replacement. She had the dating apps in a locked folder on the phone, so I never got to see everything, but I knew she had the apps and for the few days I had her phone, she got messages like constantly."

"Were there any that stood out?" Lucas asked.

Miranda shrugged. "I couldn't see the messages, just the notifications. You know *you have a new wink* or *RedTruck27 wants to connect*. That kind of thing."

Lucas nodded. "Got it. And she never mentioned any specific men in her life?"

Miranda shook her head. "Not like that, anyway.

The one who messaged her the most was Sean, wait, no, Scott. Yeah. I think his name was Scott."

Lucas looked at me, his brows lifted. "Scott Putnam?"

"Maybe." Miranda shrugged. "I told Dad that Mom was dating again, you know, to try and nudge him along."

"How'd he take that?"

"He didn't seem to care. But he asked which app she was using. I guess so he could avoid that one. Can you imagine? If they'd been matched up?" Miranda smiled. "Maybe I should have planned some kind of digital *Parent Trap*."

"You wanted them back together?"

"Not really, I guess. Mostly, I just wanted them to stop arguing over me. And part of me thought that maybe if we all moved to California, it could be a fresh start. Mom would have left her stressful job, Dad would have had his dream job, and we could have left all these problems behind. Maybe it would have worked itself out."

I smiled at the girl. Something about the wistful look in her eyes told me she knew her scenario wasn't based in reality, but it was a comfortable daydream she'd constructed for herself.

Miranda's eyes glossed over. "I guess I'm getting part of what I wished for. I just wish my mom was going with us."

I swallowed hard. "I'm so sorry, Miranda."

The teen hurried to wipe at her eyes and shook her head. "Thanks. I should get going. My dad will wonder where I am. He's been pretty protective since this all happened."

"Good luck with the move," I called after her.

She waved and then hurried up the driveway past us.

I exhaled when she was gone. "She's so young to have gone through all this."

Lucas nodded.

We got into Lucas's SUV and he started the engine, though I wasn't sure what our next move was. The dots were starting to line up, but they pointed in a direction we couldn't follow.

CHAPTER 14

Chief Lincoln was happy to see us, at least, right up until the point where we told him we'd been digging around in his murder investigation. "So, let me get this straight, you think Russell Hutchins hired a hit man fresh out of state pen to murder his ex-wife because he wanted to move to California?" he said, alternating his skeptical glance between me and Lucas like a painstakingly slow tennis match. "And you know this how, exactly?"

I drew in a breath and glanced at Lucas.

"We found a burner phone in his trash."

I blinked, surprised he hadn't attempted to sugar coat it.

Chief Lincoln kept his poker face up, but he straightened in his chair and dropped his hands to the desk, linking his fingers together.

"Uh oh, Dad's mad," Flapjack whispered.

I ignored the spectral stowaway. He'd been at the flower shop when we got back from the Hutchins' house and had insisted on tagging along to see Chief Lincoln.

"I'm not sure what you expect me to do with this knowledge," Chief Lincoln said. "If the phone was illegally obtained, I can't use it or any of its data to get a warrant, let alone as evidence in a future trial."

"Do you have the victim's phone?" Lucas asked. "She was using dating apps to meet men. It seems like it would be pretty easy to pull the information on the men she was in communication with. If Scott Putnam is among them, that should be enough for an interview, maybe a warrant."

Chief's brow furrowed. "Wait, I thought Putnam is your proposed perp."

"Yes, he is. But we think he might have gotten to Sabrina through the dating app. Her ex knew she was a member because their daughter told him about it," I explained.

"There were no signs of a break in, right?" Lucas asked.

"Nope," Chief said, shaking his head.

"So, it seems that whoever attacked her was welcome in her home. Someone like a new boyfriend." Lucas glanced at me and then added, "Do you have the victim's phone? I have the number Russ called on his burner. It's linked to an account in Putnam's name. If that number is in Sabrina's phone, that connects all the dots and brings this thing full circle."

"We do have Ms. Hutchins' phone," Chief Lincoln replied cautiously. He hesitated and drew in a breath. "We can cross reference her call logs with the number you have for Putnam, but as far as going through dating app info, I'll level with you and say we don't have the resources we need to chase down leads like that. This case doesn't even belong to our department. I'm acting as something of a backup for the Pine Shoals PD because they're even smaller than we are."

"Well then let us help," Lucas said.

"He has his PI license," I hurried to add. "Doesn't that mean he can act as a consultant? Like you do with Nick Rivers?"

Chief leaned back, mulling it over. "You have the tech to search her phone?"

Lucas nodded. "I do."

"All right. I'll give you an hour with the phone. Will that do?"

I looked to Lucas.

"I can make that work," he said. "If I turn anything up pertaining to Putnam, you'll be the first to know, Chief."

"I'll do some digging into him as well," Chief said. "Come back in an hour. I'll have the phone brought over from the Pine Shoals station."

Lucas stood and I hopped up to join him. "Thank you."

"I don't know what possessed you two to get involved in this," Chief said, shaking his head.

"Don't suppose he'd believe the devil made us do it?" Flapjack wondered.

We said goodbye and left the station before he could change his mind.

Chief Lincoln held to his word and was there when we circled back to the station an hour later. He'd had his deputies comb through the call logs and recent calls listed on Sabrina's phone but there was no record of Sabrina ever calling or texting with Scott Putnam.

Lucas took a seat at one of the empty desks in the bullpen and started going through the phone. I watched nervously over his shoulder next to the chief. Lucas worked quickly, his fingers flying over Sabrina's screen. Every few seconds, he paused to jot down information on the legal pad he'd brought along. After fifteen minutes, he twisted in the seat and handed the phone back to Chief Lincoln.

"That's it?" Chief Lincoln said, glancing at the phone resting in his open palm.

"I got what I need," Lucas said. "She kept a list of all her passwords saved as a draft in her email folder. I have the login for the dating app. So, I'll dig in and see if maybe Putnam tried connecting with her that way. If not, maybe something else will jump out at me."

Chief Lincoln gave us each a wary look but didn't voice his concerns. "All right. Keep me in the loop."

"Will do. Thanks again, Chief."

The chief's puzzled look only deepened as he slipped the phone back into an evidence bag and then shuffled to his office.

We went back to my apartment and Lucas fired up his laptop. Within minutes, we were logged into Sabrina's account and poring over the dozens of messages she'd received since becoming a member of the virtual dating service.

"Whew. There are a lot of accounts here," Lucas said.

"I'm not surprised she had a lot of interest," I said. "She was an attractive lady and she had her life together. The real question is how we're going to find out who any of these people really are? None of them use real names. It's all *B-ball4Life* and *BobcatBill68*."

Lucas started opening messages, and it didn't take long before we both felt the need to take a long shower. Innuendos, propositions, and straight up dirty talk filled the majority of the messages.

"Men are pigs," I groused, sliding Lucas a side eye. "What is wrong with your species?"

Lucas chuckled. "Hey, these guys are in a class of their own. I don't claim any of them."

He clicked to the next message and a graphic image

filled the screen. Lucas swore and quickly clicked out of it.

"Gross." I shuddered. "I'm gonna need some brain bleach to clean all that out."

"Tell me about it." Lucas soldiered on, opening and closing message after message.

I went to the kitchen and started opening cupboards. "Guess you know your place is secured, if that's what's waiting out there in single-lady territory."

Lucas laughed. "Good to know."

"So, the grocery situation around here is kind of pathetic," I said, closing the cupboards and moving to the fridge.

"I noticed that this morning," Lucas said.

"I'll run out and grab some staples while you work on thinning out the pool of creepers."

Flapjack perked. "What day is it? Friday? Hmm. They should have salmon out at the market today."

"It's disturbing that you have the fish schedule memorized," I said.

Lucas gave me a strange look.

"Flapjack."

"Figured," he said with a grin. "I'll see you in a bit."

I grabbed my purse and keys from the hook by the door and headed out to my delivery van. The market was within walking distance, but I wasn't in the mood to haul three bags of groceries back in the cold. Flapjack shimmered into the van's passenger seat.

"We're not buying any fish," I told him.

He frowned, his whiskers twitching.

"Where's Hayward tonight?" I asked once we were out on the road. "Is he out with Gwen?"

"Don't know. I didn't ask. Mostly because I don't care."

"How heartwarming."

Flapjack rolled his shoulders. "We'd be better off if he went to live with Gwen, if you ask me."

"You don't mean that."

"Why not?"

I smiled. "You can keep your little tough guy thing going if you want, but I know the truth. Hayward is your friend."

He grumbled something and stared out the passenger window. I pulled into a spot outside Thistle, Beechwood's only market, and cut the engine. "You can come with me, but I don't want any tantrums."

Good grief. Sometimes I really had to wonder about my life choices.

Flapjack went his own way when we entered the store. Pouting, no doubt. I grabbed a basket and started making a mental list in my head of everything I needed to make dinner for the next few days. Thistle wasn't a large grocery store, but they had a decent selection, and I didn't usually have trouble finding what I needed. After winding through the produce department, I cut to the cold case, grabbed some beer and a bottle of sparkling water, then breezed through the freezer section, grabbing a few bags of ready-made meals. The kind that could make me feel like an accomplished cook, while in reality all I had to do was dump a bag of flash-frozen food into a pan and turn on a burner.

There was one aisle left to go, but when I rounded the corner, I stopped short. Karla was standing halfway down the aisle, considering the ingredients label on a bottle of BBQ sauce. I tiptoed backward and bumped into another shopper.

"Watch it!" the man barked, drawing Karla's attention.

"Scarlet?" she asked.

I scurried out of the man's way and then lifted a hand toward Karla. "Hi."

"Ugh. Small towns," Flapjack muttered, appearing at my ankles. Apparently, he'd gotten his fill of fish stink for one night.

"Tell me about it," I mumbled.

Karla set the bottle of sauce back on the shelf and came closer. "I was actually meaning to call you. Is there any news on the case?"

"I'm working on it," I told her quietly. Rocking back on my heels, I glanced around the tower of boxed soda stacked at the end of the aisle. Deeming the coast clear, I leaned back in, my voice low. "Are you sure there's no way to call Sabrina back sooner? If I could just ask her a few questions things would really go a lot faster."

Karla shook her head. "I don't have it in me yet. My magic is depleted."

"Do you know anyone else like you? Someone who could summon her for us?"

"I told you I don't use my powers, so what makes you think I go around blabbing about it?"

"It was just a question."

Karla frowned. "It's not like there's an annual convention in Boca for this kind of thing, you know."

"Preaching to the choir," Flapjack interjected. "Am I right, Scar?"

I closed my eyes and drew in a slow breath.

"Don't mind her," Flapjack said to Karla. "She's just got low blood sugar."

"Flapjack! Do you mind?" I hissed.

"Not at all. But, you know how to shut me up." He grinned, flashing all his sharp teeth.

"We. Are. Not. Buying. Fish!"

Karla watched our exchange with something that looked like a mix between horror and confusion. "I have to get going," she interjected. "I'll see you Sunday."

I bobbed my head and she scurried away.

"She's odd, isn't she?" Flapjack mused.

"Pal, I don't think we have a lot of objectivity on the matter."

"Huh. Fair enough."

I grabbed a few last items and hurried through the checkout line. Lucas was still bent over his keyboard when I arrived. He glanced up as I shut the front door, and then stood to come help carry the paper bags inside.

He chuckled as he unpacked one of the bags, stacking a box of crackers and two varieties of cookies beside each other on top of the fridge. "I'm pretty sure this is the textbook example of why not to shop when you're hungry."

"You'll thank me later," I told him, ribbing him in the side as I passed behind him to toss an empty bag into the recycle bin.

"Probably. It might be a long wait before we get anything. I called my friend Daly and passed over the information for a couple of accounts I flagged. He's a computer whiz who knows how to crack databases like the one the dating site is using. He'll run down the information, IP addresses, names, that kind of thing, and pass it back to us."

"You mean, like hacking?"

"Yeah."

I cringed. "Isn't that illegal?"

"The alternative is that we pass it on to the chief, wait for him to get a warrant, and then let the dating app's lawyers battle for the protection of their clients in court. By the time that's done, the entire harbor could be crawling with demons."

I chewed my lower lip.

"One of these guys was straight-up nasty to her. Name calling and threatening her. I don't know if it's Putnam, but we need to find out who it is, regardless. Everything on the site is supposed to be secure, but if he was able to track down Sabrina's personal data, like her address ..." He trailed off, his meaning clear. "Daly will get us his IP address, and we can pass it to Chief Lincoln and let him handle it from there."

"So, what do we do now?"

Lucas reached for the cookies and handed me the box. "We wait."

CHAPTER 15

*L*ucas was out for a run when I woke up Saturday morning. I dressed quickly, scalded my tongue on a too-hot cup of coffee, and hurried downstairs to open the shop. Saturday's were Lily Pond's busiest days, tourist season or not, and Lizzie couldn't be expected to manage the whole place by herself. So, my detective cap was firmly off for the rest of the day.

By nine o'clock, I had a good head start on the day's orders and was contemplating running to Siren's Song for a second cup of coffee before opening. The side door opened and Lizzie shuffled inside, bundled in a baggy sweatshirt and a rain jacket. Her usually straight hair was up in a messy topknot and it didn't look like she was wearing any make-up. "Morning, Scarlet," she said, her tone flat.

"Hey, Lizzie. Everything okay?"

"Mhmm."

"And the award goes to …."

I leapt out of my skin at Flapjack's voice and whipped around to find him perched on the tall stool beside the work bench. I glowered at him but held my tongue. He grinned. "Morning, Scar."

Gwen popped into view next, wearing a mile-wide smile. "Scarlet! I have great news!"

"*Not now,*" I mouthed, jerking my head toward Lizzie.

Gwen's smile wilted as she dropped whatever gossip she'd been about to spread.

Lizzie hung her coat up and trudged to her work bench. She sagged onto the stool and leaned against the bench. "Scarlet, can I ask you something kind of personal?"

I rounded my own station and went back to working on the bouquet I'd been putting together when she'd arrived. "Sure."

"Well, you remember how Bryant asked me to that barbecue earlier this week?"

"Yeah. I saw you two together. You looked like you were having a good time."

"We did. He actually asked me to the movies. We were supposed to go last night. But then, like an hour before, he called and said he couldn't make it."

I frowned at the rose in my hand. "Did he give you a reason why?"

"No. And he didn't try to reschedule." Lizzie heaved

a sigh. "I think he just lost interest or maybe found someone he likes better, but then he texted this morning, so now I'm confused all over again."

"What did the text say?"

"*Hey, Lizzie. Hope you have a good day.*"

"Hmm." I looked up from the roses and studied Lizzie. "To me, that seems like a good sign. The text, I mean. But it's weird that he didn't give you an explanation for the missed date. Or at least try to make plans for another night."

She nodded, her face crestfallen. "I don't know whether he's interested or not. The whole thing is so confusing. I don't want to play games, but he's really cool and we had a lot of fun, so I don't want to overreact and mess the whole thing up."

"Did you text back?" I asked.

"Not yet," Lizzie replied, glancing at her phone. "What do you think I should do, Scarlet?"

"I'll tell you what she needs to do," Gwen started. "She needs to put on a cute dress and maybe a little shiny lip gloss, and then go over to the hardware store and show him what he's missing out on!"

I frowned at her. Yeah … that was so not the answer.

"Honestly, Lizzie, I think you should just be direct with him," I said, plucking up another rose. "Otherwise you're both stuck in this weird cycle. For all we know, he's over at Hank's, wondering if *you're* interested in *him.* So, just take the guess work out. Let him know you're open to going on another date."

"Be direct?" Gwen repeated. "Hmm. How's that working with you and Lucas and the whole ring-a-ding talk?"

I shot her a quick scowl and went back to arranging the bouquet of a dozen roses.

"Is that how you got Lucas?" Lizzie asked.

I laughed. "Oh, our first meeting was very direct. He tackled me into the grass."

Lizzie gasped. "What? How have I never heard this story?"

Smiling, I placed the final rose and then crossed the studio to grab a skein of ribbon for the vase. On my way back to my station, I paused and leaned against the counter. "Lucas was working security for that show *Mints on the Pillows* when they were here in town renovating the Lilac House. And I ... well, I was trespassing. It was dark, he didn't know who I was, so he tackled me and waved a Taser in my face."

"Ah, young love," Flapjack quipped.

Lizzie giggled. "That's a story for the grandkids someday, huh?"

I shrugged and pushed off the counter. "Maybe."

Gwen floated to stand beside Flapjack. "You've known her the longest. Has she always been this difficult?"

"She was easier before Hayward came along. I think Sir Cranky-Pants has worn off on her."

I glared at both of them.

"What?" Gwen asked.

They were lucky the iron omelet pan was out of reach.

"Tell you what," I said, placing the ribbon on the bench. "I was thinking of going out for coffee. I'll bring you back a mocha. My treat."

Lizzie perked. "Are you sure?"

"Of course!" I went into the small office and rooted through my purse to find a ten dollar bill. "Can you put a ribbon on that vase and put it in the case? The card's on the front counter with the order slip."

Lizzie nodded. "On it. Thanks, Scarlet."

"No problem." I slipped my raincoat on and tucked the ten dollars in my pocket. "Be back in a few."

Gwen and Flapjack floated out after me.

"*Now* can I tell you the news?" Gwen asked.

I sighed. "All right. What's up?"

"Well, you remember how we didn't find any ghosts in Pine Shoals?"

I nodded.

"Hayward thought it was weird, so we went back this morning, early, and it turns out there are ghosts there, but they have this weird thing of only coming out at night."

"Why?"

"I don't know. They're strange, to say the least, but we found one who haunts Sabrina's neighborhood and you're never going to guess what she told us!"

I stopped walking. "She saw the murderer?"

"No, but she said there was a strange van parked across the street from Sabrina's house almost every night for a week before the attack. And she has the license plate number."

"Gwen, this is huge! Why didn't you say something sooner?"

She shrugged. "I tried, but Lizzie was there and you told me to keep quiet."

"Gwen, you should have told me it was about the case! I thought you were there to tell me something went amiss with Ms. Marshall's perm or that some celebrity had a baby."

"Why would you think that?" Gwen asked.

"I—I—oh, never mind." I shook my head and dug in my jean's pocket for my phone. "What's the plate number? I'll text it to Lucas and see if he can figure out who it's registered to."

Gwen told me the number and I fired it off to Lucas with a quick explanation.

"Where is Hayward now?" I asked.

"He's still in Pine Shoals, trying to see if there's anything else he can find out."

I looked down at Flapjack. "Why aren't you with him?"

For all their grievances against one another, it was rare they went more than a few hours apart.

"It's raining," Flapjack complained.

"What's your point? You're a ghost."

"Well, when you're dead, you can see if you enjoy the rain," the cat groused.

I rolled my eyes to the drizzly sky.

"I'll go see if there's more news," Gwen said.

"Thank you, *Gwen*," I said, placing extra emphasis for Flapjack's benefit.

He scoffed and stalked into the street, cutting through a passing truck before sliding into the coffee house.

"And you think I'm difficult," I muttered to Gwen.

She laughed. "Only when it comes to romance."

Frowning, I stepped off the curb. "See you later, Gwen!"

Flapjack was sitting on top of the espresso machine when I stepped inside the quaint coffee house. It took every bit of resolve not to scream at him to get down. Cassie was at the register and greeted me with a warm smile. "Morning, Scarlet!"

"Good morning, Cassie."

I ordered two large mochas and had Cassie bag up two chocolate chip scones—with Flapjacks commentary the entire time—and by the time the drinks were placed on the counter, my phone was buzzing. I stepped off to the side and pulled it from my jacket pocket. It was Lucas.

"Hey," I answered. "I'm at the coffee shop. You want me to order you something?"

"Not right now. Listen, Scarlet, I got your text and ran the plate."

My breath hitched. "And?"

"You're not going to believe who that plate belongs to. Russell Hutchins."

CHAPTER 16

I left Lizzie in charge of closing and hurried upstairs a little after three o'clock to meet Lucas in my apartment. He was dressed in jeans, a long-sleeve shirt, and his black boots. "Are you ready?" he asked.

"Are you sure we shouldn't just call Chief Lincoln? He's not going to be happy if we keep this to ourselves."

"Maybe not, but even this new link is circumstantial. Having a van outside his ex's house looks bad, but it's not technically illegal. If Chief Lincoln brings him down to the station, a guy like Russ will just lawyer up and the whole thing goes nowhere."

"What makes you think we'll get any further? He literally slammed the door in our faces last time we tried to talk to him."

"We're running out of time, Scarlet. We have to try."

"Maybe you should tell him about the ghost thing,"

Gwen suggested. "Tell him you talked to Sabrina and she knows what he did. That might rattle him into a confession!"

I shook my head. "I don't think so."

Lucas, mistaking the aim of my comment, folded his arms. "Okay, then what do you suggest?"

"No, no. Your plan is fine. You're right. I was talking to Gwen. She thinks I should tell him I can talk to Sabrina."

"Aha." He pulled his keys from one pocket and then checked the other to make sure his phone was there. "If he stonewalls us again, we'll turn the info over to the police. Although, I don't know how we're going to explain where you got the information about the van and the plate number."

I cringed. "Yeah. I didn't think about that."

Lucas drove his SUV to Pine Shoals and we parked in the same spot as the last time we'd paid Mr. Hutchins a visit. "Here goes nothing," Lucas said, killing the engine.

"I'll take the upstairs," Flapjack told Gwen and Hayward, who sat on either side of him in the backseat. "You two look on the first floor."

"I'll look in the garage. If the van's parked here, maybe I can find a clue inside," Gwen agreed.

Hayward nervously adjusted his top hat. "Be careful, Lady Gwen. And you as well, Lady Scarlet."

I nodded and threw my door open. "Let's go."

Lucas followed and we made our way up the steep

driveway. Lucas rang the bell and the ghosts slipped past the walls, entering the home without invitation. I doubted they'd find anything, mostly because none of them had Sturgeon's ability to sift through solid objects. Anything they could find would have to be out in plain sight and I doubted a man like Russelll would be sloppy enough to leave definitive proof out in the open.

Still, it kept them busy and it certainly couldn't hurt things.

The door opened, and Miranda appeared on the other side. "Oh, hello, again."

"Hello, Miranda. We are actually here to talk to your dad. Is he home?"

"Um, sure. Let me go get him. What was your name again?"

"Scarlet," I said.

"Okay. Do you want to come inside and wait?"

I glanced at Lucas and he nodded. "Sure. Thank you."

She led us into a sitting room off the foyer but neither of us took a seat. Miranda smiled and then ducked out to go find her father. My nerves cinched tighter with each passing moment, and when Russ finally stormed into the room, I felt like a Jack-in-the-Box about to burst out of my own skin.

"What the hell do you think you're doing?" he growled, fire flashing in his eyes. "I have half a mind to call the cops and have you both arrested for trespassing, but I don't want to scare my daughter. She's been through enough!"

"Go ahead and call the police, Russell. We'd love to share with them some of the information we've dug up in the last few days about your involvement in Sabrina's murder."

Russell swore. "For the last time, I had nothing to do with her death!"

"Prove it," Lucas said. "Answer our questions."

Russ hesitated.

Lucas held his hands out. "Listen, we can either deal with this here and now, or we can pass along this information to the police and you can spend your whole day down at the station answering their questions. You'll have to call a lawyer and make a whole thing of it. Or, we can just have a quick conversation."

Russell glanced over his shoulder and then moved further into the room, dropping his voice low. "You have five minutes, so start talking."

"Here's what we know," Lucas began, his tone commanding. "You had a burner phone that you used to communicate with Scott Putnam, a violent felon. Those calls stopped once Sabrina was murdered. Then a van, registered to you, was spotted outside Sabrina's home for several nights right before the murder. Of all the people the cops have looked into, you have the strongest motive, by far. You were bleeding money to pay alimony and child support, and even with that, Sabrina wouldn't agree to let you alter the custody agreement so you could accept a new job offer and move out of state. With her gone, all of those problems vanish, virtually overnight. So, you tell me, why should we believe you when you tell us you had nothing to do with this?"

Russell ran a hand over his jaw. "Scott Putnam is a piece of human trash. The reason I was calling him was to tell him that if he didn't leave Sabrina alone, I'd personally see to it that he found his way back to a prison cell. I used a burner phone so he couldn't trace it and come here to my house. I called him one time after Sabrina died. I thought maybe he was the one who killed her. He didn't answer so I threw the phone out."

"Did Sabrina ever meet him in person?" I asked.

"No. He messaged her on some app. My daughter told me Sabrina was dating again. I didn't have an issue with that. It was her life, right? I asked Sabrina about it, just to make sure she was being careful and to keep it away from Miranda going forward. That's when she told me about this Putnam guy. They'd texted a little, but then he got weird and she cut it off. I asked her for his number and told her I'd take care of him. As far as I know, they never took it past exchanging phone numbers."

"Did you tell the police? Afterward, I mean?"

Russ shrugged. "Sure, I told them about Scott. They didn't seem interested, but said they'd look into it."

"Why not tell us this yesterday?" Lucas asked.

Russ eyed him. "Sabrina's parents didn't need to know about it, that's why. That's who hired you, isn't it?"

"No, actually."

"Then who did?"

"It doesn't matter," Lucas replied, his tone leaving no room for argument. "What about the van outside Sabrina's house?"

"That was me," Russ admitted, a little reluctantly. "I wasn't stalking her or anything, but I pass her street on my way home from the office and sometimes ... sometimes I'd stop by and think for a little while. Sabrina and I had our issues, but I loved her. Still do, I suppose. She's always going to be Miranda's mother, my first ... well, everything. That's not something you can just shake off because you aren't together anymore."

Russ paused, his gaze drifting past us to the large window at our backs. He sighed and shook his head slowly. "I still can't believe she's gone. Now, all I've got is a truckload of regrets. All the nasty things I said. My affair. I—" his voice broke off and he drew in his lower lip. After a moment, he collected himself and nodded. "I screwed things up, and I can't help but think, if I hadn't, none of this would have happened. She wouldn't have been home alone that night. I would have been there. Where I was supposed to be."

My heart clenched tightly and I reached for Lucas's hand.

Russ dragged his eyes back to us and he crossed his

arms. "Does that clear everything up? I have a lot of work I need to get back to."

"It does," Lucas said with a small nod. "Thank you for your time."

"We're sorry for your loss," I added.

Russ inclined his head and then led the way back to the front door.

Lucas and I plodded back down the drive to his SUV in silence, each reeling from the candid conversation. We climbed back into the vehicle and buckled back into our seats, tension and disappointment clouding the air between us.

Finally, Lucas exhaled slowly and glanced over at me. "Well, that was a bust."

I tried to shove aside my building panic, but it filled my chest anyway. "What do we do now? We're back to the beginning, and we have less than twenty-four hours."

"Tomorrow night this Summoner can call Sabrina back, right?"

I nodded. "Assuming she hasn't been eaten by a demon."

Lucas swallowed hard. "Right. Well, maybe speaking with Sabrina will help us get a new lead. We don't know that this portal thing is going to open quickly, right? We might still have plenty of time."

"I really don't know. I didn't know demons were a thing until a few days ago."

Lucas snorted. "Guess we're both learning a lot this week."

Guilt nipped at me. "Right."

We hadn't formally talked about the supernatural bomb I'd dropped on him prior to his visit.

"I should have told you about Holly and all the rest of it a lot sooner," I said. "If it makes you feel better, I only learned about witches and werewolves and all that since moving to Beechwood Harbor."

"Really?"

"Well, I knew there were forces and weird, unexplainable stuff. I mean, I see ghosts!"

Lucas chuckled. "I guess that is one hell of a tip off."

"Kind of hard to ignore." I smiled. "I mean, I've met all kinds of spiritual practitioners in my travels. I was searching for answers about my gift and I spoke with witch doctors and priestesses. All kinds of different religious gurus, but this ... this is a new ballgame for me too."

"What do you say to a *no more secrets* policy?" Lucas asked.

I smiled. "Fair enough."

Gwen, Hayward and Flapjack trooped out of the Hutchins' home, scattered a few minutes apart. None of them found anything incriminating and I recapped the conversation we'd had with Russ.

"So, he's officially off the suspect list?" Gwen asked.

I nodded. "Looks like it."

"So, that leaves us where?"

"Screwed," Flapjack answered.

I frowned at him. "Thanks for that."

"Hey, just speaking the truth."

"Scott Putnam still looks good for it," I said, thinking aloud. "He obviously has a history of violence, and there's now a formal connection between him and Sabrina. The only issue is how he found out where she lived and why Sabrina would have let him into her house at night if he was someone she'd blocked from the app."

"Maybe he opened a new account and tried again, using a catfish approach?"

Flapjack perked. "Catfish?"

I sighed. "It means pretending to be someone else online."

Lucas's phone rang. He glanced at the screen and then sat up a little taller in his seat. "Oh, hold on. This is my buddy, Daly. He's been digging into the info on the dating app. Maybe he's got something on Putnam."

He lifted the phone to his ear. "Daly, one sec, I'm gonna put you on speaker so Scarlet can hear too." He lowered the phone, tapped the screen. "Can you hear me?"

"Copy that."

Lucas grinned. "Good. Please tell me you have something?"

"I got an address for one of the accounts you flagged," Daly said.

"Which one?"

"It's *RedTruck27*. He was one of the guys sending her those terrible messages, calling her a slut and stuff. Really abusive crap. Sabrina blocked him from contacting her, but I was able to get his account information anyway."

"Is it Putnam?" Lucas asked.

"I don't think so. Unless he lives right next door to your victim."

"What do you mean?" Lucas asked.

"If I have this right, the guy sending the worst of the messages lives next door to the address listed in Sabrina's account settings."

"You got a name?" Lucas asked.

"Barry Wentsworth," I whispered.

"That's right," Daly confirmed.

Lucas turned over the SUV's engine and peeled out.

CHAPTER 17

"This doesn't make any sense!" I exclaimed as Lucas sped through the streets of Pine Shoals, following the GPS on his dash as it spouted directions back to Sabrina's neighborhood. "Why would Barry kill Sabrina? They were friends. He was taking her soup that night because she was sick."

"That's what he told you," Lucas replied. "We don't know if that's true."

"I told you something was off with that guy," Flapjack interjected from the back seat.

"Like Daly said, he was sending Sabrina messages in the app. Obviously using a different alias."

"He's the catfish!" Hayward declared proudly.

"Stop talking about fish. You're just making me hungry," Flapjack grumbled.

Lucas took the final turn, and we were on Sabrina's old street. I pointed at Barry's home. A For Sale sign was stuck in the grass outside Sabrina's house. I flung my seatbelt off before Lucas even set the parking brake. "To think, I sat there in his living room and drank his coffee, all while he lied to my face about being Sabrina's friend!"

"To be fair, I don't think you actually drank any of the coffee," Flapjack said.

"Let's go see what he has to say for himself," Lucas said.

We went to Barry's door, ghosts in tow, and I pounded on the door. Barry peeked out the narrow window beside the door. His brow creased but he opened the door. "What's this all about?" he asked. "Are you writing another article?"

"Article?" Gwen asked.

"That was her cover," Flapjack explained quickly.

"Aha."

"I believe you'd make a fantastic journalist, Lady Scarlet," Hayward chimed in.

Ignoring the ghosts, I kept my eyes trained on Barry. "I just have one more question for you."

Barry faltered, glancing nervously at Lucas. "I see. Well now's really not a good time. I was in the middle of tidying up..."

Flapjack laughed and proceeded to slip inside, sliding past Barry's ankles. Gwen and Hayward followed, not taking as much care. Barry shivered as they passed through him. "I—I suppose I could put on some coffee."

Lucas glanced at me, and I offered a small nod. "All right."

We entered the cluttered home. Lucas's eyebrows raised when Barry turned his back to go into the kitchen. "This is cleaned up?" he whispered.

I glanced around and then shook my head. To me, it still looked like I'd walked onto the set of a *Hoarders* episode.

A coffee maker kicked on and Barry reappeared in the living room. He didn't look openly hostile, but his curiosity bordered on annoyed. "What is it you want to know?"

"It's very simple, Barry. I'd like to know why you lied to me about your relationship with Sabrina."

"What are you talking about?"

"You were a member of the same dating app and you were using that as a shield, hiding behind a fake name and photo to harass her."

Barry flinched. "I did no such thing!"

"Does anyone else live here?" Lucas asked, looking around. "Or use your internet?"

"No."

Lucas continued, "The IP address being used to send the messages was coming from your house. How can you explain that if you weren't the one sending them and no one else had access to your connection?"

"Sabrina was dating again," I said. "She was single. You're single. Maybe you had a crush but didn't know how to bring it up. So, when you found out she was on a dating app, you joined too. What happened, Barry? What made you turn on her? Did she reject you?"

Something sparked in Barry's eyes. "She never gave me a chance."

"How did you know about the app?" I asked.

"She was bringing men home every time her daughter was gone. It was a different one every time. They'd stumble in drunk and laughing. I mentioned it once and she told me she'd signed up for this service and that I should try it."

"Why the fake account?" Lucas asked.

Barry licked his lips. "I never planned on meeting anyone. It was stupid. I was curious. That's all. I found a photo online and made up a name. I messaged with a few women and I ... I don't know, it spiraled out from there."

"Did Sabrina message you?"

Barry hesitated, a debate warring in his eyes.

"Did she flirt with you the way she flirted with those other men?" I pressed.

"We messaged every night! We could talk for hours. I was thinking about telling her the truth, coming clean. I asked her how she felt about me and she told me she was devoted, that she wasn't seeing anyone else since she met me."

Something shifted, the tension in the room ratcheting up another level.

"What happened next, Barry? Did you tell Sabrina who you really were?"

"I don't want to talk about this anymore. Why is this any of your business?" Barry demanded, taking a step backward. "Why do you know things about IP addresses and dating sites? Who are you?"

"Hey, Scar, you might want to check this out!" Flapjack said, hurrying into the room from down the hall. "He's got a whole shrine of photos, some of them ... indecent. Hayward's in there on the verge of a panic attack. I didn't see it last time because he had the closet doors closed."

I glanced down the hall and took a step.

"Where are you going?" Barry snapped.

I took another step.

"You can't go down there!"

I looked at Lucas and then bolted. I raced down the hall, following on Flapjack's heels. Hayward and Gwen stood on either side of the closet—Hayward with his back turned. I gasped and Lucas's heavy footsteps followed.

"No!" Barry shrieked.

There were personal, intimate photos of Sabrina. Ones she'd clearly taken herself. Then, there were others, photos taken of her sunbathing in her backyard, wearing a bikini. I'd never seen Sabrina's yard, but I would have bet anything that the angle of the camera lined up precisely with Barry's own yard, perhaps through a gap in the fence just large enough for a camera lens.

"What did you do to her?" I asked, my voice shaking

as I stormed back out to the living room. Lucas blocked the opening of the hallway and Barry looked ready to self-combust, his face bright red.

"I'll call the police!" he bellowed.

"No." I shook my head. "I don't think you will. Then you'd have to explain those pictures in your room. I think they'd be especially interested in the ones you took from your side of the fence."

"You want to know what happened to Sabrina? She got what was coming to her, that's what! She showed up with some guy just after telling me she was only chatting with me and that she thought I was something special. She was a liar and a slut!"

"So you killed her?" I asked, my voice just above a whisper as the pieces clicked together in my head. "You decided that if you couldn't have her, then no one else could either."

Barry scuttled across the room, shoved a pile of garbage off the dining table, and revealed a small handgun. He swung around, leveling it at me. "You need to shut up! You don't know what you're talking about. And if you try and tell the police any of this nonsense, I'll blow your head off!"

My hands shot into the air. "Barry, please, don't shoot!"

"Drop it!" Lucas said.

Flapjack launched himself into the air and things moved so fast it was like a blur. Flapjack let out a terrible yowl and a string of violent hisses. Barry screamed. The gun flew from his hands and hit the floor with a loud *bang*.

Lucas sprang into action when the gun went flying, tackling Barry to the ground. Barry screamed. "You broke my arm!"

"You just pointed a gun at my girlfriend's head. You're lucky you have any bones left intact," Lucas growled.

"Flapjack, are you okay!" I asked, going to the ghost's side. He lay still, his eyes roving the ceiling. "How did you do that?"

"I—I don't know. I just knew I had to do something and I ... I did."

"You were amazing! You just saved my life."

"Who is she talking to?" Barry asked as Lucas hauled him to his feet.

"None of your business," Lucas barked. He didn't have cuffs, but he was a lot bigger and stronger than Barry and was easily keeping his arms pinned behind his back as he frog-marched him to the kitchen.

I heard duct tape being ripped off a roll.

"Surprised lover boy could find anything in this dump," Flapjack said, sputtering slightly.

"What happened?" Hayward

"I just saved Scarlet's life while you were in there crying over seeing a blurry nudie pic," Flapjack grumbled.

"I was not crying," Hayward argued.

Gwen dropped beside the cat and stroked his fur. "Are you okay, Flapjack?"

"Yeah, yeah, I'm fine." He pushed to his feet and flicked his tail around a few times.

"Cops are on their way," Lucas called from the other room.

I rose to my feet and went to the kitchen. Lucas had Barry fastened to a chair with the tape. I glowered at him. "Are you even sorry for what you did?"

Barry glared at me, refusing to answer.

Moments later, a harsh knock sounded on the front door. "Pine Shoals PD, open up!"

I went to answer it, and two officers came inside, weapons drawn. I gestured at the kitchen and they went ahead.

"We'll be outside," Gwen said.

I nodded. "Thank you."

Chief Lincoln arrived to the scene twenty minutes later. Barry was sitting in the back of a squad car, screaming even though no one sat in the front seat to hear his protests. Lucas and I stood on the sidewalk, having given our stories to the responding officers.

"This place is going to be a nightmare to search," Chief Lincoln said, circling back out to us after he'd gone inside for a quick look. He exhaled and then started ordering the deputies into action before he took our official statements.

As I wrapped up my own statement, a deputy approached Chief Lincoln and held up two plastic bags. "The hem of this t-shirt is ripped up. Thinking maybe she grabbed ahold during the fight. Might be able to pull her DNA from it."

I swallowed hard and Chief Lincoln waved the deputy off. "I don't understand what makes people do terrible things like this."

"I don't either," he replied. "I doubt I ever will."

"How do you do it, Chief? How do you look this kind of evil in the face and keep fighting? Doesn't it wear you down?"

"Of course it does, from time to time, but it's worth it. Overall." He considered me. "You going to tell me what got you tangled up in this investigation in the first place?"

I smiled. "Just doing my part, I guess."

He didn't believe me, nor did I expect him to. "Well next time, how about giving me a call *before* you go charging into a suspect's house, hmm?"

I laughed. "Fair enough. It's a deal."

CHAPTER 18

Karla already had the summoning circle laid out when I arrived at the funeral home on Sunday evening. Gwen, Hayward, and Flapjack were all in tow and Karla eyed them when we trooped into the viewing room. Flapjack was still gloating over his heroic moment, replaying it like a sports highlight. Lucas had some questions about the whole thing, but I honestly didn't know what to tell him. Flapjack had never had the ability to interact with the physical world, but in that moment, sheer desperation had channeled his energy into a force strong enough to knock the gun from Barry's hands.

"I saw the paper this morning," Karla said quietly. "Looks like we have something to offer Sabrina."

I nodded. "Barry's not getting out of jail anytime soon. He gave the police a full confession in hopes of getting a cushier prison assignment. I just hope news of his arrest is enough to help Sabrina let go of this plane."

Karla inclined her head. "Only one way to find out."

She slipped the necklace over her head and placed it in the circle, speaking the same incantations as the first time. I wasn't sure how it all worked, and honestly, I didn't want to, but it was clear the necklace was the key that opened the window to the other side.

The lights glowed, forming the circle. Gwen and Hayward gasped and recoiled to the wall, going as far as they could without slipping through into the adjoining room.

"Relax, you two," Flapjack said. Glancing at me, he added, "I told you we should have left them at home."

I shushed him and nudged my chin at Karla. Her eyes were closed and she spoke Sabrina's name and the date of her crossing. Some kind of Otherworld ID system, apparently.

The lights pulsed and Sabrina's faded form came to stand in the center of the circle. Ghosts didn't age the way humans did, but there was something strained in her eyes that made it appear as if she'd aged ten years since the first time Karla summoned her forth.

Guilt pricked at me as I approached her. "Hello, Sabrina."

"Please, tell me you've come to set me free," she said, her voice strained. "I can't do this much longer."

"I'm so sorry, Sabrina. Listen, we don't have long, but I wanted to let you know that we've solved your murder. The man who did this to you is in jail now, and he won't be getting out again."

Sabrina looked startled by the news. Her gaze ping-ponged between Karla and me. "Who—who was it?"

I drew in a breath. "It was Barry Wentsworth."

Sabrina frowned. "Barry? You're sure?"

"He confessed to the whole thing, and the police found enough evidence to make the case a slam dunk. Chief Lincoln thinks he'll plead guilty and skip the trial altogether."

"Why?" Sabrina demanded, anger edging her tone. "Why would he kill me? I was never anything but nice to him!"

Karla shot me a concerned look.

"It appears he harbored feelings—um, romantic, feelings, for you. And when it became clear that you didn't share those feelings, he decided either he was going to have you or no one would."

Sabrina's expression relaxed, recognition dawning in her haunted eyes. "My date! That's what this is about?"

"Barry said he saw you with a man," I confirmed.

"A few months ago, I started online dating. I hadn't dated since college, when I met Russell. I was being cautious. But the night before, well … Miranda was staying with her father and I had the house to myself. I went out on the fourth date with this man I'd been seeing and when it was over, I invited him home. He was the first man since—well, since the divorce." She paused her story and gave an irritated toss of her head. "That's what this was about? He had a crush?"

Her pain was palpable, surging through me as she connected all the pieces together. "I'm sorry, Sabrina. It's senseless and horrible."

She chewed her lower lip. "I still can't remember that night."

"It's likely for the best," I told her. "You don't need to. What matters now is that the man responsible will be put away for the rest of his life, and when his time comes, he won't find the same peace that's waiting for you."

The thought seemed to comfort her slightly. She nodded and wrapped her arms around herself. "I can leave this place, now? I don't like it here. I'm alone and all I can do is think."

Karla looked at me expectantly and then glanced at her watch.

I held up a finger. "There is one more thing," I interjected, aware we were running out of time. Lucas's number was already queued up on my phone. I pulled it from my back pocket and with a single tap, called him. I let it ring twice before hanging up.

"What's going on?" Karla asked, her eyes narrowing. "Is someone here?"

I drew in a breath. "Sabrina's daughter."

Karla's eyes snapped wide again. She looked at the ghost penned in the circle.

"My daughter?" Sabrina asked, her voice cracking.

"Is it okay?" I asked Karla.

She didn't look overjoyed, but she dropped her chin, giving a single nod.

I stepped into the hall and waved Lucas and Miranda inside the viewing room. They'd been waiting outside the front doors of the funeral home until I gave the signal by calling Lucas's phone and hanging up.

"Are you sure you're ready?" I asked Miranda.

The teen nodded, wisdom beyond her years reflecting in her eyes.

Lucas inclined his head. "She's ready."

"Okay. Remember, we don't have a lot of time." I stepped aside and ushered them into the room.

Sabrina sobbed at the sight of her daughter. "Miranda!"

The teen cautiously entered the room, taking tiny steps closer to the summoning circle. "Mom?" she whispered. "It's really ... *you*?"

Sabrina nodded fervently. "It's me, baby girl."

Miranda leaned forward, not quite a foot from the circle. For a moment, I thought she might inch closer, but she remained in place, as though an invisible hook held the back of her shirt.

Sabrina's eyes shone with silver tears. "You look so beautiful. How are you?"

"How—how is this *real*?" Miranda asked, her eyes darting to Karla and me.

"I'll explain later," I told her. "Remember, we can't hold the connection for too long."

Miranda looked back at her mother. "I miss you."

Sabrina wiped at her eyes. "I miss you, too. I'd give anything to be there with you again. But, you're going to be all right. You're strong, and I know you're going to do great things with your life."

A tiny smile pulled at Miranda's lips.

"You listen to your father. He's going to drive you crazy, but he loves you, and he only wants the best. Try to remember that. I'm sorry for the things I said about him. That wasn't fair of me to put you in between us."

"It's okay, Mom."

Sabrina sniffled. "Do your best in school. You're so smart, baby girl. Don't ever let anyone tell you otherwise. And never, ever give up on your dreams. Life is so short. Treasure the little things. It's not always going to be fireworks and butterflies. But there's something in each day worth celebrating, so look for it. Okay?"

Miranda nodded, swiping her own tears away.

"And remember, I'll always be there, watching over you from this side. This isn't goodbye. It's a see you later."

Sabrina smiled at her daughter, her eyes still glossy, but they'd lost the haunted quality they'd had when she'd first appeared. She looked ... restful.

Almost happy.

Her silvery form flickered and she surged upright and a bright light flashed. When it faded, Sabrina was gone.

"Did we run out of time?" Miranda asked, whipping around to look at me and Karla.

I smiled sadly and shook my head. "She moved on. She's at peace now."

Karla shot me a surprised look. Without a word, she closed her eyes, whispered a spell and waited. When her eyes reopened, she looked at me. "How did you know?"

"I've seen it before. This time felt different."

A sob slipped from Miranda's lips and she crumpled. I rushed to her side and gathered the girl in my arms, holding her as she cried.

For all my time working with ghosts and those they'd left behind, I still wasn't good at knowing the right words to say. So, I remained quiet as I held the teen until she quieted.

"Thank you," she whispered when she pulled out of my arms. She sniffled and wiped her eyes, smearing her mascara and too-thick eyeliner. "I'm glad I got to see her again. Really. It means a lot."

Even as more unshed tears glistened in her eyes, I could feel her release some of the pain she'd been carrying. She'd never fully get over losing her mother—no one ever did—but she had some semblance of closure and got the rare opportunity to hear her mother's parting words of wisdom, something many must yearn for.

"You're welcome, Miranda. If you ever need

someone to talk to, please call me. You have my number."

She nodded and gave me a quick hug before thanking Karla.

Lucas placed a hand on Miranda's shoulder and escorted her outside. He'd take her home and then meet me back at the shop. When the front door of the home fell closed, I exhaled slowly and pivoted back to Karla. "Thank you for helping me."

"I'm glad it all worked out." She sniffed and started gathering the items from the circle, starting with the necklace. "I'm also glad you learned your lesson before you could do too much damage. Imagine what would have happened if you'd sent more than one ghost on before they were ready!"

"Believe me, the thought has kept me awake more than once this weekend," I said sourly.

Karla placed the last item into her canvas satchel and tucked it under one arm. She considered me for a long moment.

"What?" I asked defensively. "I swear, I'm not going to do it again! You don't have to worry about me."

"No," she said, "it's not that. I was just wondering how you do it."

"Do what?"

"This," she replied, gesturing around the room. "Dealing with ghosts, taking on their pain and problems. It must be exhausting."

"It has its moments," I agreed. "But, I figure I was

given this gift, by whatever power or force in the universe, and I should use it for good."

"I used to," Karla said quietly. "When I first realized what I could do. It became my obsession, my whole world. I opened my home to anyone wanting to speak with their dead relatives. Once word got out, there were people who'd travel from all over the country, then the world, to meet with me. The demand was relentless and eventually, I was forced into being a prisoner in my own home, afraid that the moment I poked my head out, someone would be begging for help."

"What happened?" I asked.

"I ran away in the middle of the night. I packed up my car in the dead of night, put a note on my front door, and drove away. I lost everything. My job, my friends. Most of my family members think I'm insane." Pain flickered across Karla's face. "It was horrible. I kept driving until I hit the coast, found Beechwood Harbor, and decided this was as good a place as any to start over."

"What led you to working here? Of all the places, this seems risky. I mean, if you're trying to avoid the dead altogether, a funeral home seems an odd choice."

Karla's lips formed a wistful smile. "I suppose it is. It happened somewhat by accident. There was an opening for a receptionist and I took it. I had enough money to last a lifetime, thanks to the years spent hosting seances, but I needed a reason to get out of the house every day. I was afraid of turning back into a hermit, I guess."

"Maybe there's a reason you chose this place," I suggested. "You're still drawn to the work of helping those mourning a loss. But now, you do it without overextending yourself and your power."

Karla considered it and then shrugged. "Maybe. The owner always said I had a knack for the bereaved. That's why she promoted me to manager and now leaves the place in my hands while she's off enjoying her retirement."

"Well, for what it's worth, I've seen you in action, and I'd have to agree."

Karla inclined her head. "Thank you."

I sighed. "I'm envious of your ability to draw boundaries, in a way. I do my best to keep my involvement contained to a single evening, but somehow it always seems to get away from me and turn into an all-encompassing disaster."

Karla looked past me, and I didn't have to turn around to know she was searching the faces of Hayward, Gwen, and Flapjack. "I don't have advice for you, Scarlet. If you can find a balance, I wish you well, but personally, I've found it too difficult to live with one foot set in the world of the living while the other remains planted in the world of the dead."

And only one of those worlds was one I could leave.

CHAPTER 19

Karla's words tugged at me long after we left the funeral home and returned to Lily Pond. I tried to tamp them down, but they proved resilient to my efforts at banishment. The trio of ghosts kept me company as I puttered around the shop, watering the potted plants, sorting out the cards and gift displays that had gotten out of order during the frenzied week.

Eventually, Hayward and Flapjack went upstairs, bickering about what to watch on TV later that night. Gwen lingered behind and glanced at me. "They're so impossible sometimes."

I arched a brow. "Sometimes?"

She laughed quietly.

"You and Hayward seem quite cozy these days," I said, smiling at her. "Things getting serious?"

Gwen fidgeted with one of her feather earrings,

peeking up at the ceiling. "Nothing official, but I think he's getting ready to ask me to be his girlfriend, or whatever Old English term he'll use." She smiled. "And when he does, I think I'll say yes."

"That's great! And also, it's about time," I said, winking at her.

"He's something special," Gwen said. "That's for sure."

"He is."

Karla's words needled at me again. It wasn't possible for me to walk away and leave Gwen and Hayward and Flapjack behind. If someone came to me and told me they could remove my magic, ridding me of ghosts altogether, the offer wouldn't hold a drop of temptation. Not anymore.

"You know, there's something I still don't understand about Sabrina," Gwen said, floating up to sit on the front counter while I dusted and wiped down the credit card machine and computer keyboard.

"What's that?" I asked her.

"Was it that we solved the case or that she got to see her daughter that helped her move on?"

"I'm not sure," I replied, stilling my duster to consider it. "Maybe a little of both?"

Gwen nodded slowly. "It doesn't really matter in the end, I suppose. Sabrina can now rest in peace, and I'd say her daughter can move forward a little easier, too."

I ran the duster over a stack of impulse-buy items in front of the register. "I hope so."

"You made it happen, Scarlet. You gave them the best gift imaginable, all things considered."

"I know. Though, I can't help but wonder what might have become of Sabrina if she'd stayed as a ghost. Maybe she would have come to love it in time. Then she could have watched first hand while Miranda grew up."

Gwen wrapped a strand of her shiny hair around her finger. "No one can say for sure, of course, but I've been a ghost for over forty years now. I've met dozens, maybe even a hundred other ghosts in that amount of time. Some just seem ready to go. They don't want to stay here, and to them, each day is a long slog. Keeping her here when she didn't want to be, well, in my opinion that would be worse. In my opinion, anyway."

"What does it feel like for you then?" I asked.

"I think of myself like a humming bird," she said with a smile. "I buzz through every day and when the sun goes down, I'm always surprised that another day is gone so soon."

I smiled at her. The analogy was quite fitting. Gwen flitted from place to place, like a happy hummingbird on a busy summer day. She wasn't to be pitied or hurried along. She was thriving. Maybe someday that would change. And if it did, I hoped I would be there to usher her into whatever waited on the other side. Though, I had a feeling she'd outlast the rest of us by a long shot.

"What about Hayward?" I asked. "Somehow, I can't picture him as a hummingbird."

Gwen laughed softly. "He tries to keep up with me sometimes, but we know we're different types of ghosts at the end of the day. Between you and me, I think he's afraid to move on. He's grown quite stodgy hasn't he? Or maybe he was always that way."

"I don't know," I replied thoughtfully. "I mean, when we met, he begged me to let him tag along because he wanted to travel and see the United States. That's a pretty big leap."

"That's true." Gwen nodded. "Sometimes it's hard for me to picture him like that. I think maybe he just didn't want to be alone anymore."

My heart squeezed at her earnest assessment. It rang true.

"He saw something in you, something he could trust." Gwen paused, her smile widening. "Although, he knew you were a package deal with Flapjack. So ... maybe I'm way off."

My head dropped back as a belly laugh bubbled up. "To be fair, Flapjack took it a lot easier on him in the beginning."

Gwen laughed. "That's even harder to imagine!"

"Tell me about it. If only I knew then what I know now!" I teased.

"You'd still do it all the same, wouldn't you?" Gwen asked. Something about the look in her eyes told me she already knew the answer.

I nodded. "I would. You three are my family."

"That means a lot, Scarlet." Gwen's eyes shone silver. "Thank you."

Something stirred within me and I opened my arms to her. Gwen's eyebrows lifted. I leaned forward, and ever so gently placed my arms around her neck. She gasped and then embraced me back, tighter than I would have anticipated based on her slight frame.

"How is this happening?" she breathed.

I didn't answer. I didn't know how it all worked, and now more than ever, I was convinced I never would, but I'd reached the place where the answers no longer mattered.

All that mattered was what was there, in front of me, and that was love.

Logic or explanations were secondary.

THINGS SETTLED back into a steady groove. Business was slower than during the peaks of tourist season, but I enjoyed the less frantic pace, especially as it afforded me the ability to take most Saturdays off to either drive to Seattle or host Lucas when he drove into town. His new job was going well, and he'd even started looking at houses a little ways outside the city limits. Seattle was still too far for my taste, but we were making the long-distance work as best we could.

I still held my weekly ghost meetings, but each time the familiar faces gathered in the shop, I couldn't help but hear Karla's parting words echo through my head. We hadn't seen each other since the night Sabrina crossed over. I'd sent Lizzie to do the deliveries to the funeral home the last few times. I didn't have ill feelings toward Karla, but thinking about the encounter only reminded me that I had a decision to make. I couldn't live forever torn between two worlds. My new powers opened the door into the spirit world even wider and it was up to me whether I wanted to step through it or not.

By October, I'd made up my mind and asked Gwen to call a special meeting. On a chilly Thursday night, everyone assembled in the flower shop at seven o'clock. Gwen had asked multiple times for a hint as to what the meeting would entail, but I knew that telling her would essentially be putting a bullhorn up to my lips and broadcasting it to the whole ghost community, and negate the purpose of holding a formal meeting in the first place.

When the last stragglers floated in, I took my place behind the counter and cleared my throat loudly. A dozen pair of eyes shifted my way, and a hush fell over the small crowd. "I know you're all anxious to find out why I've called you here tonight, so I'll cut to the chase." I glanced at Gwen out of the corner of my eye.

Hayward stood beside her. Flapjack hadn't been able to resist his own curiosity and perched on a high shelf beside an arrangement of collector tea cups, observing from afar.

"Many of you have heard about what happened with Sabrina and Loretta earlier this summer. I'm sure there are many rumors and partial truths attached to the story by now, so I'll set the record straight. I did play a part in ushering both women over to the other side."

I paused as a swell of excited whispers rippled through the crowd.

"However, it's not something I plan to do again. It's dangerous and I'm not comfortable risking it, regardless of how ready the ghost might feel. If I've learned anything from the experience, it's that there is a natural order, or cycle, to this whole thing and it's not my place to interfere with it. Just because I *can*, doesn't mean I should, and as was the case with Sabrina, my involvement nearly ended in disaster."

"How did you do it, Scarlet?" Perry, one of the elderly gents in the crowd, asked.

"I'm not entirely sure how my powers work, and that's why I've called you here today," I replied. "As much as I've loved getting to know each of you, I think it's time we draw this group to a close."

The whispers turned frantic.

"Let me clarify," I continued, holding up my hands to try and quite the speculation. "I think the support group should continue. I'm not closing it down, more like removing myself from the equation."

"But why?" Alyssa, a younger ghost in the front, asked.

"I think my role in this cycle has come to an end. Most of the time, I just listen anyway. I'm not really doing anything. I don't know what it's like to be in your shoes, to be a ghost. You all help each other way more than I ever could, because you understand one another on a level I can't."

"So, you're just trying to get rid of us, is that it? We're an inconvenience now?" another voice in the back shouted.

"No! That's not it at all. You're free to use this space as long as you'd like, every Tuesday, just like before. But in my place, I think a new leader should take the reins." I glanced sideways. "Gwen? Would you come forward?"

Gwen touched her chest, clearly startled, but she swooped toward me and turned to face the crowd. "Me, Scarlet?"

I nodded. "Gwen, you're the most compassionate and perceptive person I know. You see people as they truly are, and you have a heart of gold. Without you, this group wouldn't even exist. You might have brought people here to see me, but the real heart and soul of this group is you."

"But what about you?" she asked softly. "Are you leaving?"

"No," I replied. "I'll be around. But for some time now, my life has been divided, split right down the middle, trying to navigate through two worlds that would never truly meet. Add in a long-distance relationship and a small business and it's more than a little overwhelming. I still need to fully figure out my magic and find my purpose, but I don't feel I can do that while trying to keep up with everything else."

Gwen nodded. "I understand." She looked to the crowd. "We all do. Sure, it's been a while for some of us, but we can all remember how crazy life gets. So, if Scarlet needs some time away to process and make plans for her future, we can give that to her, can't we?"

With some hesitation by a handful of members, the group agreed and even grew enthusiastic after a few moments of consideration.

Smiling, I took Gwen's hand and squeezed. "Thank you, Gwen."

"It's an honor."

Things died down after another half an hour, and the group dissolved, ghosts leaving in pairs and small groups until it was just the four of us again. Flapjack leaped down from his high shelf and landed without a sound on the counter. "Well, that could have gone sideways. You nearly had a ghost mutiny there, Scar."

Gwen laughed. "I have to admit, I'm more than a little surprised that was your announcement. But I understand why you need to take a step back. You've had a lot on your plate for a long time now."

Hayward approached, his top hat in hand. "This doesn't mean you're sending us away, does it, Lady Scarlet?"

"Of course not," I told him.

I shot Gwen a quick grin and then rested one hand on Hayward's shoulder. It took him a moment to realize what had happened, but he jumped when he put the pieces together. "Lady Scarlet!"

I laughed and removed my hand. "A new little trick I picked up somewhere along the way."

Flapjack looked the most stunned by my new ability. He crept closer and I extended a hand, remembering the way I used to stroke his fur when I was just an ordinary little girl and he was my beloved kitty cat. Slowly, he lowered his face and brushed his cheek against my hand. It wasn't the same warm fur coat I remembered, but there was a comforting tenderness in the gesture all the same.

"You guys are stuck with me," I said, smiling in turn at my three constant companions.

I wasn't sure where the next steps on my journey would lead, but it was nice to know I'd never be alone.

CHAPTER 20

"Where's Gwen when you need her?" I muttered, staring at my reflection in the full-length mirror in Lucas's master bedroom. I tottered, shifting from foot to foot, trying to compare two pairs of heels. On my left foot, I wore a black pump that featured a pencil-thin stiletto spike and on the right, a peep-toe slingback with a much lower heel. One was good for walking—well, okay, *better* for walking—while the other made me feel like a fashion model.

That is, when I wasn't wobbling like a newborn giraffe.

"Peep-toes for the win," I said, kicking off the left shoe. Two minutes in the stilettos and my toes were already crying.

Maybe it was better Gwen wasn't here to advise me. She would have voted for the stilettos, hands down.

Smiling, I put on the other slingback and then clicked across the hardwood floors to the attached bathroom to finish getting ready. I had to admit, it was fun to get dolled up every now and again. I spent my life in jeans, leggings, and faded t-shirts, and in place of nail polish and makeup, I usually had green stained nails and the only thing on my face was a slight sheen of sweat.

Lucas had recently returned from a two-week trip to London and had planned a special dinner to celebrate his return from another successful business trip. He'd made reservations somewhere but was being vague about the details. I assumed he was planning another fancy night out like after he'd received his sign-on bonus and was dressing for the occasion. If we ended up at a drive-thru, I was gonna kick him in the shins.

I glanced at my reflection one last time, double-checking every detail. My copper hair was lighter than normal, with golden highlights peeking through thanks to all the time I'd spent in the sun over the summer. My makeup wasn't too extreme, but I liked the healthy glow of my skin and the way the eyeliner made my eyes look a little wider.

Thank you, YouTube.

Satisfied, I turned off the lights and set out to make my grand entrance. After all, the big reveal is the best part.

Lucas was in the kitchen, his back toward me. I stopped and cleared my throat.

He jerked upright and whipped around, one hand in the front pocket of his navy slacks. He wore a matching jacket and a button up shirt and tie. "Scarlet, wow! You look amazing." He crossed the kitchen and took one hand, leading me through a silly twirl. He whistled as I spun back to face him. "I was about to send a search party in after you, but it looks like you knew exactly what you were doing."

I laughed. "A search party? It's been an hour and a half." I cringed, spotting the digital clock on the microwave over his shoulder. "Okay, *two* and a half. Are we late for our reservations?"

He smiled. "I built in some extra time to get a drink. So you are right on time." He kissed me. "Shall we?"

"Yes, please. I'm starving." I took his offered hand and he led the way toward the door. "Can I get a hint about where we're going? At least what kind of food? I need to set my appetite."

Lucas chuckled and opened the front door. "Sorry. No dice. You're just going to have to wait."

I stuck my bottom lip out. This only made him laugh harder.

We went down the hall to the bank of elevators, and Lucas pressed the UP button.

"Wrong button," I said, gesturing at the panel.

He smiled. "It's the right one."

My brow furrowed. "We're going *up*? Did they install a cafe on the roof since my last visit?"

He chuckled and wrapped an arm around my waist. "Guess you'll have to wait and see."

"What are you up to?"

He kissed the tip of my nose.

The elevator buzzed, announcing its arrival, and we boarded. Lucas slipped a key from his pocket and inserted it into the button marked PH.

"Penthouse?" I said. "Are we going to a party?"

Lucas refused to answer, only offering a mischievous wiggle of his brows.

I sighed and he chuckled.

A soft ding announced our arrival and the doors slid open. Lucas guided me off the elevator and two doors down the hall. He used the same key to open the door and ushered me inside.

The luxury penthouse was alight with what had to be a thousand candles, all surrounding a table set for two in the empty living room that was all the more breathtaking with the two story wall of glass windows. Soft music played from speakers hidden somewhere in the room, filling the huge space with a jazzy tune. On the table, a bucket of ice held a bottle of champagne, and there was a bouquet of flowers in the center of the table, showcasing all of my favorites.

"Lucas, this is beautiful." I turned around to face him. "But what are we doing here? Who's place is this? You didn't buy this … did you?"

Lucas chuckled. "No. This place is a little out of my price range. My boss actually owns it, but he's put it on the market and offered to let me use it for tonight. You're not going to find views like this except maybe at the top of the Space Needle."

"It's stunning."

He came to stand beside me and drew me to his side. "I'm glad you like it."

"And the candles and flowers? Champagne? What's the occasion? You're not buttering me up to tell me you're leaving on another trip so soon, are you"

"No," he replied with a soft chuckle. "I don't have any big trips scheduled until the spring."

"Okay, so then—"

The doorbell rang before I could pepper him with a second round of questions. Lucas pulled away from me and went to answer it, and I followed a few steps behind. When Lucas opened the door, one of the building's staff members appeared, holding a large pizza box. "Here you are, sir."

Lucas stepped away to thank the young man and slip him a handful of bills.

The staffer gave me a quick nod and then ducked out of sight.

"What's this?" I asked, as Lucas turned back, pizza box balancing on one palm.

I read the lid of the box and frowned. "Wait, that's the pizza shop in Beechwood. How did you—"

"I had them freeze it for me. Take and bake style," he

explained, moving to set the pizza on the table. Steam rose from the pie as he lifted the lid. "I had the restaurant downstairs do the honors. It's the same pizza we had—"

"—on our first date," I finished, a lump of emotion swelling in my throat.

"Don't you mean our first *not-a-date* date?" he teased.

"Did I miss our anniversary?" I asked hesitantly. I wasn't always the best with dates like that.

Lucas chuckled, shaking his head. "No. This is something of a new anniversary, I'm hoping."

I tilted my head. "What are you up to?"

He looked at the table. "I was thinking we should eat first, but if we do that, I might lose my nerve, so I'm just gonna do this. Now."

"Lucas?" A flutter of anticipation quivered through my stomach.

Lucas was rarely ruffled, and standing there, hands in his pockets, he looked uncomfortable. A glisten of sweat shone on his forehead as he shifted his weight. "Scarlet, I've been in love with you since the night we shared this same pizza, in the kitchen of that haunted house, talking about the world and traveling, and well, the crazed ghost."

I smiled, conjuring up the memories of the evening. "You mean, it wasn't love at first tackle?" I asked, grinning as I reminded him of our initial meeting.

He laughed and reached for my hands. "Scar, that

was the best tackle I ever made in my life. I should have scooped you up right then and carried you off."

"That's very caveman of you, but go on," I teased.

He licked his lips. "I think about our future all the time. More so, now that I'm here in Seattle. I finally feel like I have a home base. It's like all the dots are connecting, especially now that I'm out looking at houses, but every time I go on a showing, I'm seeing more and more that there's still one thing missing."

My breath caught in the back of my throat and I held it tight.

Lucas smiled at me, his eyes glossy. "I can't imagine a forever without you in it. I don't know what adventures lay ahead in the future, but I know there's no one else I want at my side for whatever may come. So, what do you say we make this thing official?"

I drew in a quick breath as he dropped to one knee.

Lucas fished a small box from his pocket and popped it open, revealing a stunning art deco ring with a cushion-cut emerald, flanked by natural diamonds in a yellow-gold band. "Scarlet Sanderson, will you marry me?"

His question spiked a dozen of my own. Where would we live? What about my job? His job? What would my parents say? If I moved to Seattle, what would happen to the ghosts?

I looked up from the ring and locked eyes with Lucas. All of the questions disappeared, leaving only an answer in their place.

"Yes!"

Lucas stood, gathering me in his arms for an earth-shaking kiss. As we parted, a burst of cheering and applause erupted over my shoulder. I jolted in Lucas's arms and twirled around to find Hayward, Flapjack, and Gwen standing behind me.

"What are you guys doing here?!"

"Aha, I take it our special guests have arrived," Lucas said.

I looked back at him. "You knew they were coming?"

"Who do you think invited them?" he replied, a gleam of mischief in his eyes.

"But how?"

He chuckled. "I had a little help from your friend Holly."

A surprised laugh bubbled from my lips. "Did you tell her you know she's a witch?"

"Not exactly, though she likely figured out you spilled the beans. You might get an interesting phone call tomorrow."

I laughed and looked at the three smiling faces. "Thank you, Lucas."

He kissed me again, and then I turned back to face the ghosts, holding onto his side. "Well, what do you guys think?" I asked, flashing my new ring.

"Scarlet, you're engaged!" Gwen squealed, surging forward to inspect the ring. "You have no idea how hard it's been to keep this a secret for the last three weeks!"

I laughed. "Three weeks? Whoa!"

"Don't kid yourself, Blondie. Every ghost in a ten mile radius of the harbor knows about this," Flapjack interjected. "Literally the *only* person you didn't tell was Scarlet."

"Well that's technically the only person that mattered," Gwen insisted, souring at Flapjack's accusation.

Hayward wedged between then, placing one hand on Gwen's shoulder. "You were splendid, my dear." He leaned in to take a gander at the ring and then tipped his hat to Lucas—not that Lucas could see. "Quite a beauty, young man. Well done!"

"Does this mean he's officially off the scoundrel list?" I asked.

Lucas blinked. "Scoundrel?"

I laughed. "Hayward's a little protective."

"I'm happy to admit when I'm mistaken, Lady Scarlet. You have my blessing."

I looked at Flapjack. "What about you?"

Flapjack looked past me and up at Lucas. After a moment, he shrugged. "I guess he'll do. He's not overly annoying."

I laughed harder. "Well, that's the Flapjack gold-standard." Turning back to Lucas, I grinned. "Looks like it's official. We're engaged!"

Lucas wrapped me up in his arms. "Then I'm the

luckiest man in the world. Tonight and every night I get to spend with you."

Tears pushed past my lashes as I squeezed my eyes closed and held him tight. Everything was going to change, but I'd never been more sure of the path beneath my feet. With Lucas by my side, forever, there was nothing I couldn't handle.

Ghosts included.

THANK you for reading Big Ghost's Don't Cry. I hope you had as much fun reading Scarlet's latest adventure as I had writing it. Of all the characters, Flapjack certainly has the loudest voice—not that this comes as a surprise to anyone—and always has me laughing along as I go. It was great to revisit Scarlet's spooky wonderland. Scarlet's next adventure just might be her biggest yet! Find out what happens next in Diamonds Are a Ghost's Best Friend.

. . .

Going to the chapel and we're gonna get ... haunted?

I've got a ring on my finger and a date circled on the calendar, let the wedding planning begin!

As luck would have it, the little wooded chapel I've got my heart set on is plagued by the not-so-nice spirit of a former bride. She died on what was meant to be her wedding day and isn't going to step aside to let anyone else take her place at the altar. She claims the chapel is cursed and points to her own murder as a sure sign, but I'm not convinced.

I'll have to keep my new reaper powers in check and solve this case the old-fashioned way if Lucas and I have any shot at starting our happily ever after underneath the majestic pines.

Download Diamonds Are a Ghost's Best Friend today!

Sign up for my newsletter to make sure you're the first to know when I have a new release, promotion, or fun freebies! You get two prequels just for joining, so head over to my website to get signed up now. www.DanielleGarrettBooks.com/newsletter

If you can't get enough Beechwood Harbor and want to chat about it with other readers, come join the Bat Wings Book Club on Facebook. It's my happy little corner of the internet and I love chatting with readers and sharing behind the scenes fun.

If you're enjoying Beechwood Harbor and want more bite-sized adventure with Scarlet, Flapjack, Holly, and the rest of the paranormal pals, you'll love Betwixt Volume I. This collection is packed full of "in between" stories. You just might meet a new friend!

Until next time, **happy reading!**
Danielle Garrett
www.DanielleGarrettBooks.com

ALSO BY DANIELLE GARRETT

One town. Two spunky leading ladies.
More magic than you can shake a wand at.
Welcome to Beechwood Harbor.

Come join the fun in Beechwood Harbor, the little town where witches, shifters, ghosts, and vamps all live, work, play, and—mostly—get along!

The two main series set in this world are the Beechwood Harbor Magic Mysteries and the Beechwood Harbor Ghost Mysteries.

In the following pages you will find more information about those books, as well as my other works available.

Alternatively, you can find a complete reading list on my website:

www.DanielleGarrettBooks.com

SUGAR SHACK WITCH MYSTERIES

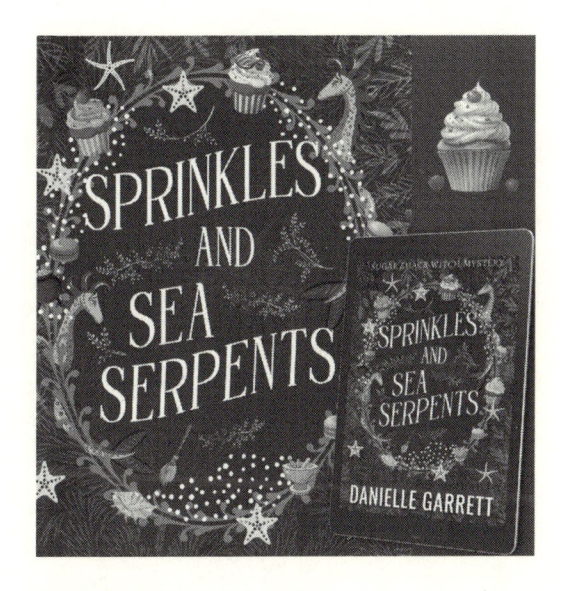

In Winterspell Lake there are things darker than midnight...

Sprinkles and Sea Serpents is the first book in a brand new paranormal cozy mystery series by Danielle Garrett. This series features magic, mystery, family squabbles, sassy heroines, and a mysterious monster hunter—all with a little sugar sprinkled on top.

Find the Sugar Shack Witch Mysteries on Amazon.

MAGIC WITH CAT-TITUDE

Cora Hearth just inherited her Aunt Lavender's sassy talking cat. What a lucky witch.

This series of laugh-out-loud paranormal mysteries is perfect for anyone who wanted to adopt Salem the cat from *Sabrina the Teenage Witch*.

Check it out right "meow" and get ready for a hiss-terical magic ride!

ABOUT THE AUTHOR

Danielle Garrett has been an avid bookworm for as long as she can remember, immersing herself in the magic of far-off places and the rich lives of witches, wizards, princesses, elves, and some wonderful everyday heroes as well. Her love of reading naturally blossomed into a passion for storytelling, and today, she's living the dream she's nurtured since the second grade—crafting her own worlds and characters as an author.

A proud Oregonian, Danielle loves to travel but always finds her way back to the Pacific Northwest, where she shares her life with her husband and their beloved menagerie of animal companions.

Visit Danielle today at her website or say "hello" on Facebook.

www.DanielleGarrettBooks.com

Made in United States
Troutdale, OR
12/03/2024

25623416R00142